SONS
OF THE
DARK

outcast

Also in the

SONS OF THE DARK

series

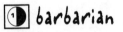 barbarian

 escape

SONS OF THE DARK

3

outcast

LYNNE EWING

VOLO

HYPERION/NEW YORK

First Edition

1 3 5 7 9 10 8 6 4 2

Printed in the United States of America

Library of Congress Cataloging-in-Publication Data on file
ISBN 0-7868-1813-1
Visit www.volobooks.com

For Jack Ewing

E

A.D. 1989

very seat in the emergency room was taken. Patients with gunshot wounds and chest pains lined the walls. It was a normal crowd for a Saturday night in Los Angeles, but even so, the neonatal nurse couldn't get used to the chaos in that part of the hospital. She sucked on a menthol cough drop, hoping to blot out the smells, although past experience had taught her that nothing could effectively cover the stench of illness and death in the trauma center. She had tried to avoid working down there, but the doctor on duty needed someone to help care for an abandoned newborn.

She entered the examining room and approached

the surgical table, where the infant lay sleeping inside the wicker basket in which he had been found. She started to pick him up, but when she touched the gray blanket wrapped around him, a shock raced up her arms. She drew back, startled, and a frightened, intuitive voice told her to run. Where had such a thought come from? She had always prided herself on being sensible and unflappable. She took a deep breath and ignored the apprehension tightening around her. What harm could a newborn cause? She picked up the baby and gently removed the blanket.

His umbilical cord had been clamped, and his skin felt warm. She carried him to the scale and marked his weight: six pounds, two ounces. But when she started to measure his length, she paused, then turned, sensing movement behind her.

The basket was gone. She thought it must have toppled, but when she walked to the other side of the table, the basket wasn't there. Perplexed, she looked back, and her jaw dropped. A coarsely woven red blanket now swaddled the newborn. She spun around, determined to scold whoever was wasting her time with practical jokes.

But common sense told her no one could have

come into the room, covered the child, and left without being seen. She hurried toward the entrance anyway. A doctor stood at the nurses' station talking on the phone, and three patients lay on gurneys.

Slowly, she turned back. Except for the infant, she was alone in the room. She refused to give in to the fear racing through her and dutifully removed the red blanket. This time, the cold air made the baby shriek. She started to lull him with a song, but the melody caught in her throat as a strange vibration coursed through her arms and forced her to set the newborn down. She backed away from him, feeling dizzy with both terror and awe.

A soft halo quivered about the child as thick threads spun around him, weaving another blanket, metallic blue this time.

CHAPTER ONE

KYLE PUSHED his way through the dancers, trying to find his three roommates. He wanted to leave before another fight broke out. He had come to Luna Moth so Obie could check out the drummer in the new band Invent, but now Kyle had a bad feeling. He had lived with Berto, Samuel, and Obie long enough to know they were keeping something from him.

Another song began with blistering energy. Clubbers swept around Kyle, spinning him into their dance. Slithery black leather gloves and gossamer sleeves grazed his sweaty face and neck. He liked the carnival atmosphere here, and part of him wanted to stay and party, but he didn't have time to join the fun.

Over the bobbing heads, he spotted Berto near the exit; Berto's strong features looked tense under the pulsing red lights from the Christmas trees set up on either side of the door. Samuel and Obie stood beside him, scanning the dance floor, as if they didn't want anyone to see them leave. Kyle knew they were going to ditch him. They had been trying to get away from him all night.

He should have known it would end that way, with the three of them turning against him. He had tried to help them adjust to life in Los Angeles and stay out of trouble. It hadn't been easy. They made fun of his fear of the authorities, but Kyle understood what one official could do to ruin a person's life. He had grown up in foster homes and had endured frequent upheavals as a boy, living in strangers' houses, some good, some not. Except for Mrs. Caine, there was no one from his childhood who even cared what happened to him.

A dancer collided with Kyle, knocking him into a girl with long black hair. She whipped around. Her canine teeth had been filed into fangs and her dress looked medieval.

"Sorry," Kyle muttered, trying to ease past her.

The metal tips of her finger armor dug into his arm, pulling him back. Her boldness surprised him.

"I haven't seen you here before." She smiled up at him, flicking her surgically sliced tongue. It darted in and out, forked like that of a snake. She grabbed his hand and turned it, studying his palm as if she were going to read his fortune.

"Were you in a fight?" she asked playfully.

He followed her gaze. In the dim light, the paint stains on his knuckles looked like bruises.

"Oil paints," he said, glancing anxiously at the door. His roommates were starting to leave. "I'm working on a self-portrait."

"I've modeled before." She caressed his hand and tilted her head provocatively. "Do you want to paint me?"

"It would mean hours in one pose." He studied her, and then brazenly swept his fingers through her glossy hair. His mind was racing, imagining her pose, but then he glanced up and saw the door close behind Samuel. He had to go after his roommates. "Sorry," he said. "But I can't."

She dropped his hand, his rejection seeming to fuel a rage in her. "Go back where you belong."

"Where's that?" Kyle asked. He hadn't *belonged* for as long as he could remember. Everyone called him a loner.

"Any place but here," she said, and she let her body fall back into the throng of dancers. A guy caught her, then two more, and soon the clubbers had lifted her and she was floating over the crowd, carried on a sea of hands.

Kyle pressed forward. He had gone only a short distance when someone tugged on his shirt. He swung around and froze.

Emily stood behind him, looking lost and out of place among the more Goth crowd. Her inviting smile confused him. They shared the same biology class at Turney High School, but she hung out with the popular kids and was always too busy with her friends to talk to him.

"What are you doing here?" he asked, but then he remembered her best friend, Maddie. Samuel had told Kyle that Maddie believed in vampires, spirits, and ghosts, and was determined to prove the undead walked the streets of L.A. Maybe she had made Emily join her on one of her vampire hunts. "Did Maddie bring you here?"

"Stop teasing." Emily gave him a shy look and slid her hands up his chest.

Her touch startled him. Lately she had seemed more timid than her friends, especially around guys. He thought maybe it was because of her illness. She had been sick for three months and had returned to school only in the last week.

She leaned in closer and whispered into his ear, "I like it better when you don't wear so much cologne."

He shrugged, puzzled. He hadn't worn cologne for a long time.

"Let's dance." Emily took his hand and started moving against him.

He was tempted to forget about his roommates and let them fend for themselves, but guilt kicked in, as it always did. "I'm sorry, Emily," he said, pulling away from her. "You'll never know just how sorry. But I have to find my friends."

Her mouth opened, but instead of speaking she just stared at him. Kyle turned and slammed through the kids behind him.

At the door he paused and peered outside. Fog curled thick and heavy around the streetlights and gave the night a milky glow. Kids had gathered in groups, their energy seeping into the air as if they were getting ready to riot. Security guards patrolled back and forth, trying to keep order, but already, broken beer bottles lay scattered across the road.

Kyle eased behind an old Cadillac hearse, and then crept down a path between the building and a row of closely planted hibiscus shrubs to where his roommates stood on the other side of the hedge. Through the branches, he could make out Samuel's face, and in the ghostly light, he looked distraught. Obie and Berto stood close to him talking, their voices flat and strange, as if something terrible had just happened.

"Everyone's been talking about him," Samuel said. "Maddie told me he's been playing girls, stealing them from their guys just to break their hearts." Samuel had been dating Maddie off and on since he'd arrived in L.A., but their romance was shaky. "Everyone's getting pissed off by what he's doing," he added. "Sledge and his friends are out to get him if he doesn't stop." Sledge was the quarterback on the Turney High football team, and he seemed to think it gave him the right to dole out a kind of vigilante justice to students who didn't behave as he thought they should. His best friends, Barry and Forrest, formed his posse.

"Get him?" Berto snorted dismissively. "I'd like to see anyone try."

Kyle wondered whom they were talking about. Sledge and his crew could make school life miserable for anyone who dared cross them, but something more was worrying his roommates. Even from this distance, he could sense the tension in their voices. They should have included him in their conversation. He could have given them advice and needed insight; they didn't understand the ins and outs of modern culture, and without his help, they never would.

"Allison told me the same thing," Obie added. "But I'm not convinced."

"It doesn't make sense," Berto agreed. "Why would Kyle do that?"

Kyle inhaled sharply, stunned to realize they were talking about him.

"He hasn't even dated since Catty broke up with him," Berto continued.

"But he was bitter about the breakup," Samuel put in. "So maybe—"

"He hasn't been interested in anyone, because he's still in love with her," Berto argued.

"I don't think so." Obie shook his head. "She hurt him too deeply. He doesn't even talk about her anymore."

"Even if he is over Catty," Berto continued, "why would he hook up with so many different girls?"

"He's on the rebound," Samuel said. "He's trying to escape the pain. No one likes a broken heart."

"Maybe it's something more. Something we try to forget. Could he be planning to . . . ?" Obie didn't need to finish his question; the others knew he was referring to the darkness that lived inside each of them, a hunger waiting to escape and take control.

Kyle shuddered, remembering the intense desire over which he had little control, and even now, just thinking about it awakened an aching need for that first sweet draw of breath from a victim's lungs.

"Girls have always thrown themselves at Kyle," Berto said. "He's never taken advantage of it before, so why would he now?"

"I'm just telling you what Maddie said." But the solemn expression on Samuel's face convinced Kyle that Samuel believed the lies.

"How can that be true?" Obie added. "Kyle's the one always lecturing us about right and wrong."

"I know," Berto agreed. "But he has been

up to something lately. This morning I caught him stealing money from the box, and he's been taking my bike out late at night without asking."

Kyle hadn't stolen any money. That morning he had added a twenty to their pooled funds, and he'd never taken Berto's motorcycle. He didn't even know how to ride it.

Berto raked his hands through his raven hair. "Mr. Keyes doesn't want Kyle hanging around Club Quake anymore. He thinks he's been pushing meth."

Kyle's stomach tightened. How could they believe such lies? Guy Keyes owned Quake, the most popular dance club for teenagers in L.A. Berto worked there as part of the security at the front door. He called himself the gatekeeper; he decided who was allowed to enter and who had their names placed on the clipboard. But even more important, Berto knew how to make celebrities feel comfortable.

"Nolo told me the same thing," Obie added. "And I guess he should know."

Kyle had heard enough. Nolo was the drummer in Obie's band, Pagan, but also a druggie. How could anyone trust what he said?

Kyle started back down the path, determined to confront his friends. But when he reached the last hibiscus bush, Emily blocked his way.

"Why did you ask me to meet you here if you were just going to ignore me?" she asked, challenging him. "That's so rude."

Kyle stared at her, dumbfounded. "I'm sorry," he apologized. "You must have misunderstood. I didn't ask you to meet me."

"I know what you said," she insisted. Her face flushed with a mixture of anger and embarrassment.

"When?" he asked.

"Today!" She seemed to be trying hard not to become flustered. "In class. Did you forget?"

"That's impossible," he answered, shaking his head. "I cut biology today. To go to an audition."

Her eyes widened, and then narrowed into a glare. "Do you think this is the kind of club I would go to on my own?"

He started to say no, but she didn't give him a chance.

"Is this some kind of head game you're playing with me?"

"What?" he asked, baffled, and studied her face to see if she was teasing. "Why would I do that?"

"Other girls warned me about you. I should have listened."

He started to defend himself, then paused, considering. She seemed genuinely upset, but none of what she said made any sense. Maybe she was crushing on him and this was her weird way of letting him know she wanted to hook up. But Emily could have had anyone she wanted. So why would she have chosen him?

"Well?" she said, interrupting his thoughts.

"You didn't have to make up a whole elaborate story," he answered, grinning sheepishly.

Now she was the one who looked confused. "What do you mean?"

"If you wanted to go out with me, all you had to do was ask," he continued. "I would have said yes."

"*You* asked *me*!" she shouted. "You practically begged!"

To his astonishment, she turned and walked away. He watched her shove her way through the crowd, but before he could go after her, Berto found him.

"C'mon, we're going over to Cantor's for deli." Berto acted as if nothing were wrong, as if he hadn't just moments ago betrayed Kyle.

"I'm heading back to the loft," Kyle answered brusquely. He couldn't have it out with Berto, not here. Fights were starting to break out in front of the club, which meant the cops would be there any minute. He didn't want to spend the night in a police station.

Berto stared at him. "What gives? You sound pissed."

"Why should I be?" Kyle asked, and then something inside him let go. He needed to get away before his anger turned into blows. He stepped around Berto without saying anything more and jogged to his rusted Chevy Impala. He started the engine. The tailpipe belched black smoke, and he slammed his foot hard on the accelerator.

He hated the familiar emptiness in the pit of his stomach. It reminded him of his childhood, when everyone had been against him. But he wasn't helpless now, as he had been then. If his roommates wanted to get rid of him, they didn't need to spread lies about him. His life would be easier without them. He'd leave them behind and start over.

Kyle wasn't convinced he belonged with them anyway. Berto, Obie, and Samuel believed that, together with Kyle, they were the Four of Legend, destined to fight an ancient evil and destroy its empire. But the other three had mysterious powers, while Kyle had none. Berto could go into a trance and leave his body. Obie was a rune master who cast spells, and Samuel used totems to call forth power animals. So far, Kyle only had the keen ability to pay bills and hook up the Internet, and he'd never seen anyone ward off supernatural creatures with a credit card.

He parked his car in the lot behind the

apartment building as the metro rumbled overhead on its last run through Chinatown. He headed toward the apartment and rode the elevator to the top floor.

The light on the landing had gone out again, leaving the hallway darker than the night outside. Kyle fumbled with his keys and unlocked the door, but as he started to go inside, he was stricken with an odd feeling that someone was watching him. He turned back and saw nothing that should have made him feel uneasy. But past experience had taught him to trust his instincts. For the first time that he could remember, he locked the door behind him and slipped the dead bolt into place.

As a child, he had been afraid of the dark, because he heard things moving about in his room. He had believed his toys came alive after the lights went out, but now he knew the darkness hid greater dangers. Another universe paralleled modern-day Los Angeles, and sometimes things from that world crossed over into this one.

He and his roommates were Renegades, fugitives from Nefandus, where they had been enslaved. Bounty hunters were trying to capture them and take them back for a reward. Could one be stalking him now?

Kyle stood frozen, unable to move. Maybe one had followed him and was waiting somewhere, hidden in the loft. It wasn't the first time he had encountered creatures from the other side, but he didn't understand why this time his courage had left him. He only needed to turn on the light to see who was in the room with him, but his hand clutched the doorknob as if to anchor him in the entryway. He began to tremble, suddenly realizing he didn't want to see what was in the room with him.

A furtive whisper broke the quiet. "Kylie-Kyle-Kyle." Someone called his name in a familiar, singsong manner, dredging up memories Kyle fought to forget.

"Who's there?" he asked, hating the stutter in his own voice.

Silence followed, and then footsteps thudded across the unfinished floor, echoing in the cavernous room. Kyle recognized the uneven tread and was cast back into childhood again.

He had spent many nights nestled under his covers in the dark, listening to someone pace back and forth at the foot of his bed.

His heart pounded, and his mouth went dry. He held his breath, listening, but what had been there was gone. Had it only been his imagination? He stepped to the light switch and flicked it on. Three bare incandescent bulbs blazed, but the glaring brightness didn't calm his nerves. His palms sweated, cold and clammy from panic. Then a draft swept through the room. Someone had opened the back door. The bright orange electrical cords swayed, twirling the lightbulbs and making shadows dance across the walls.

Kyle strode forward, nervously studying the corners and doorways. Bounty hunters were also shape-shifters. They could dematerialize into shadows and float, a black mist across the sky; but so could Kyle—all *servi* could. That had been the normal mode of transportation in Nefandus. He started to release his body in case he was forced to flee, but stopped, sensing something else.

Beneath the smells of linseed oil and turpentine, he detected another odor that didn't belong. He breathed the fragrance of bitter oranges. When nightmares had awakened him as a child, his room had been filled with the same scent. He tried to reassure himself that someone had brought home oranges, and rotting fruit was the source of the pungent smell. But as he started toward the kitchen to investigate, he glanced at the self-portrait he had been painting, and his blood went cold.

Someone had altered his work, subtly shifting the expression on the face. Kyle stepped closer to the easel, examining the wet paint and brushstrokes. He had been trying to capture his loneliness and longing, not his rage. He couldn't remember adding the furrows to the forehead or the angry lines around the eyes, but even if he had, why would he have tried to make himself look so evil?

Maybe one of his roommates had been playing around with his paints, but he doubted it. The artistry was too delicate; only a few brushstrokes had dramatically changed the appearance. An amateur couldn't have done that, and the style was clearly his. He rubbed his temples, trying to calm the throbbing pain. He had no recollection of changing the portrait, but before he could consider it more, the sound of a creaking floorboard interrupted his thoughts. Someone was in the room with him.

CHAPTER TWO

SHADOWS RIPPLED behind Ashley, still entwining her hair, as if she had just materialized. She had once been a *serva*, but she had betrayed her own kind and, after escaping Nefandus, had become a *venatrix*, a bounty hunter, granted freedom to come and go between the two worlds. She took off her sunglasses and smiled at Kyle.

Her tender gaze surprised him, but he knew not to trust her. He stumbled backward, wondering where she had been that she needed dark glasses at midnight, and then he breathed the cloyingly sweet smoke clinging to her clothes and recognized the scent from the magic fires that burned in Nefandus. She had just returned from the other side.

She stepped toward him, her hips swaying. "Is that the greeting I get?" she asked when he continued to back away.

"What do you expect?" he said, searching the room for any shimmer of air that might warn him that others were coming through with her.

"Don't you trust me yet?" she teased playfully.

"Never," he answered.

"Why are you acting so jumpy?" Ashley started to embrace him, and he put up his hands, keeping her back.

"It's my normal reaction when I'm around you," he answered.

Ashley looked at him curiously. "I hope you mean that as a compliment."

"Don't you remember what happened the last time we tried to be together?" he asked, wondering why she was coming on so strong. Their past romance had not ended on a friendly note. Kyle had been crazy in love with her once—or maybe the feeling had just been infatuation. She had a way about her that could make any guy fall for her. "Why would I ever trust you again?"

"Things are different now." Ashley pulled away and looked around the room, her hands gliding over the table where he kept his sketches, brushes, and paints. She appeared to be searching for something. "I have feelings for you."

"At least look at me when you lie to me, Ashley."

She spun around. "Why would you think I'm lying?"

"Because you always do."

"Those games are over." She returned to him and wrapped her arms around his waist, lifting her face for a kiss.

He unhooked her arms, even though he craved her embrace. Ashley couldn't be harmed by his kiss, as other girls could, because she had been a *serva*. Like him, she had been trained to feed on souls. The hunger was just one curse put upon all *servi*, so that if they did escape back to the earth realm they would never find happiness in their freedom; they would always be a danger to others, forced to live apart or destroy anyone they loved. Kyle wondered how many souls Ashley had taken. He doubted that she even tried to control the darkness inside her, and he didn't understand why that should make him feel sad.

"What's wrong?" she whispered, caressing his back.

"Berto is my best friend," he said, and this time it took all of his willpower to push her away. "I won't do this to him."

"That didn't concern you last night," she answered dreamily.

"Last night?" For the fourth time in as many hours Kyle felt as if he had fallen into a hole. Was she telling the truth? Ashley was known for her manipulative behavior, but Emily would have had no reason to lie to him, and, for that matter, what could his roommates gain by spreading rumors about him? Then he glanced at his self-portrait. The changes in his painting, more than anything, made him wonder if he could be doing things and not remembering.

Finally, he spoke. "Last night I was going over my lines."

"And I was helping you," she answered, running a finger down his cheek. "Dissolve with me."

He was tempted. A pleasant ache rushed through him as he remembered the luxury of drifting over the city, looking down at the lights and cradling Ashley's shadowy apparition against his. As dangerous as she was, there was also something irresistible about her, something deeper than her beauty. At one time, he had thought that she could be the perfect mate for him, but their romance had been a deception. She had been using him. "Not tonight," he answered, pulling away.

She scowled. "You promised we'd—"

Kyle placed his hand over her lips before she could finish. The back door had opened, and now the sounds of footsteps and voices came from the kitchen.

"Go," Kyle said. "My roommates are home. I don't want Berto to see us together."

"Why?" Ashley asked. "He's got to find out sometime." She appeared to enjoy the power she still held over Berto's emotions—and over Kyle's.

"Damn it, Ashley." Kyle shoved her behind him as Berto entered the room.

"It's not what you think," Kyle said abruptly.

"What do I think?" Berto paused near a window, and Samuel joined him.

"Ashley likes to stir up trouble. She craves drama and—" Kyle stopped. His speech had become rapidfire, his voice nearing panic.

Berto frowned, but his scowl wasn't from jealousy; he looked baffled.

Kyle spun around. Ashley had vanished. When he turned back he caught the quick exchange of anxious looks between Berto and Samuel.

"Why are you bringing up Ashley?" Berto asked. "I told you she was a closed case."

Kyle felt the lie in Berto's words. Everyone knew he still loved Ashley.

"Just . . . I don't know." Kyle raked his hands through his hair, trying to settle his nerves. "I guess I was thinking out loud."

"We got takeout," Samuel said, gazing

uneasily at Kyle. "It didn't feel right eating at Cantor's without you since it's your favorite."

"Thanks," Kyle said and followed them into the kitchen. He wasn't going to confront them now about their conversation outside the club. It could wait until morning. At the moment he felt too confused. He needed to eat, clear his head, and think over everything that had happened that evening.

"Dig in," Obie said.

Sandwiches were set out on place mats made from folded brown paper bags. A plastic bottle of orange drink anchored one corner of each sack, and jars of mustard sat in the middle of the table, near a large bowl of fries.

Kyle sat down and took a bite, relishing the spicy taste of hot pastrami.

"You've changed since our last trip into Nefandus," Berto began slowly. His sandwich sat untouched in front of him. "Did something happen to you there?"

"You saw it," Kyle answered, wiping his mouth on the dish towel they used as a shared napkin. "A Regulator almost destroyed me. If

Samuel hadn't changed into his power animal, I wouldn't be here." Kyle remembered the Regulator holding him, leaching his strength, and he wondered if contact with the Regulator could have released toxins into his system. Maybe poisons had caused a slight brain injury. Something he hadn't really noticed until now. Could that be why he wasn't remembering things he had done?

"Kyle?" Berto's voice penetrated his thoughts.

"Yeah?" Kyle looked up. His roommates were staring at him again, their faces strained with worry.

"Are you all right?" Obie asked.

"Sure, why not?" Kyle answered and took another bite. But the food felt like cotton in his mouth, and he had to take a swig of orange soda to wash it down.

"The last time we went into Nefandus we didn't run into Regulators," Berto said. "Not one."

Kyle felt as if the room had tilted. He put his sandwich down. "We were captured and taken to the coliseum. I remember it clearly. Hundreds of Regulators were participating in the ceremonies. All of Nefandus was there to watch the blood sport."

The others looked at each other, and the silence became unbearable.

"What?" Kyle asked.

"Our last journey was three days ago," Samuel said finally. "We went to the dig where I had been enslaved. We'd planned to steal the black diamond. Do you remember what that is?"

"Of course I do," Kyle answered, hating Samuel's pathetically condescending tone. "It's a wish-granting gem that has power over all the magic in the universe."

Samuel stared at him then shook his head and looked away.

"What?" Kyle demanded.

"Did you drink something while we were there?" Berto asked. "Maybe you took a sip of water, something that could be affecting you now?"

Kyle shook his head. "I don't remember

going into Nefandus three days ago," he confessed at last.

"You have to," Obie said. "It was your idea. You led us."

CHAPTER THREE

"**Y**OU'RE KIDDING." Kyle stared at his roommates, overwhelmed. "I'd remember something as important as that." But even as the words came out, he was no longer sure.

Berto started to say something, but Kyle stood up and left the room.

In his bedroom, Kyle picked up his drawing pad and a stick of charcoal and flung himself on his bed. He began sketching to clear his mind, trying to make sense of everything that was happening. But could he even trust his own thoughts?

His first reaction had been anger, but now he felt frightened. If his roommates were telling the truth, then maybe he was suffering from some kind of memory loss, possibly a delayed reaction to the potions he had been forced to drink in Nefandus. He didn't feel disoriented or drugged, but something was definitely amiss.

He knew that under severe stress people sometimes developed short-term amnesia. They were conscious of their actions at the time, but later, when they returned to their normal state, they had no recollection of what they had done. Was that happening to him?

His stress level had been high and climbing. Recently the reality of his predicament had set in: he'd never be able to live a normal life or fulfill his dream of becoming a famous actor. In Nefandus, all *servi* were given immortality, because slaves were more valuable if they remained young forever. So how could he become an actor? Fans would eventually notice that he never aged, and what would happen then? He felt doomed to an eternity of moving from town to town, changing high schools and trying to fit in. His stomach churned just imagining sitting in geometry class, century after century, but what else could he do?

And, unlike the Immortals who lived in Nefandus, *servi* were not given the ability to regenerate. So if he stepped in front of a truck, he would continue to exist, a mangled body, alive and sentient.

But trying to adjust to immortality was just one problem. His roommates were another. When Kyle had left Nefandus, he had returned to his own time in modern-day Los Angeles, but the others had been kidnapped from different eras. Berto was a Toltec from the year 1000 A.D. Obie was a barbarian, a member of the Goth tribe, and Samuel's home had been the eighteenth-century American wilderness. When they escaped, they had assumed they would return to their own worlds. Instead, all three had found themselves trapped here.

Kyle felt sorry for their plight, and even though he didn't show it, he cared for them. They needed him, and right now he needed them even more. He started to get up to go back to the kitchen, but they were already standing in his room, forming a semicircle around his bed.

"I didn't hear you come in," Kyle said.

"You've been too preoccupied lately," Berto said.

"And acting strangely," Samuel added and lifted his hands, showing Kyle he meant no offense.

"I don't feel any different," Kyle answered, surprised by the tremor in his voice. "But if everything you're saying is true, then I've got some serious problems."

"We want to help." Obie wrote a line of runic letters across the air. "This incantation will make you remember."

The archaic words glowed and swarmed around Kyle in a wreath above his head, spilling golden dust. Kyle blinked, feeling a surge of warmth. He remembered where he had left his gym clothes the month before, but that was all.

"Sorry," Kyle answered Obie's expectant look. "I don't remember our last trip to Nefandus."

"Maybe I need to work a stronger incantation." Obie started to wiggle his finger again, but Berto grabbed his wrist and forced his hand down.

"You might make things worse," Berto warned.

"Make what worse?" Kyle asked, anxiously studying his friends' faces. His heart dropped. "How can there be more you're not telling me?"

"We think your power is trying to express itself and you're forcing it back," Samuel said.

"If I had any kind of ability, I'd let it out," Kyle argued. "It's no secret I've wanted to have a power like the rest of you. Besides, how could I have one and not know?"

"I didn't know," Obie said and glanced down at the runic inscription on his wrist.

"I didn't have a clue, either," Samuel added, tapping the stone totems hanging on the leather cord around his neck.

"A power can be good or bad," Berto went on. "And you could be fighting yours because you're afraid of it. Maybe you sense its aggression and, as it grows stronger, you're forced to use increasing amounts of energy to hold it back. That could be creating something—"

"Like power surges that are burning up my short-term memory," Kyle finished the sentence for him. Excitement spun through him. Could he really be like the others, gifted with some paranormal ability? But then reason took over. "I haven't done anything out of the ordinary my entire life."

"You were able to escape Nefandus after only a short captivity," Obie remarked. "It took the rest of us centuries."

"I told you, a monk found me—" Kyle stopped. That in itself was odd and he wondered, not for the first time, why a man who had withdrawn from life to devote himself to prayer and solitude would live in Nefandus, a sanctuary for evil and its Followers.

"But why did the monk help *you* and not someone else?" Obie continued. "Doesn't it seem odd that of all the *servi*, you were chosen? And who is this monk, anyway?"

"No one knows his true identity," Berto

put in. "But everyone says he's helping the Sons of the Dark. Lots of people disguise themselves as him now, and that's good for us, because it makes it more difficult for Regulators to catch him."

"He must be powerful," Kyle said. "Because when we were escaping, a troop of Regulators marched right toward us. I thought we were going to be captured, but the monk told me to hide. He took off his robe without letting me see his face; then he walked over to the Regulators with this overbearing confidence, like he had a right to be anywhere he wanted, even on an escape route used by the slaves. At first I thought he was sacrificing himself so I could still escape, but when the guards saw him, they saluted. After the brigade left, the monk dissolved into shadow, so I still couldn't see his face; then he formed again inside his cloak, his face hidden in the hood."

"Whoever he is, he must have known your true identity, and that's why he helped you escape," Berto said.

"All right," Kyle conceded. "But that

doesn't explain why I'd try to repress a power if I had one."

"Maybe something happened when you were young that frightened you and made you think it was evil," Samuel suggested, "and from that time on you tried to disown it."

"I suppose," Kyle said, and his thoughts raced back to his childhood. He remembered standing off to the side on the playground watching the other children on the swings and monkey bars. He hadn't joined in and always felt like an outcast, but could his isolation have been self-imposed? Was he afraid of what he might accidentally do?

"We think that during your blackouts your power is in control," Berto said. "Maybe that explains why you're doing things that are so contrary to what you would normally do."

"You mean, it's trying to take over? To possess me?" Kyle expected his friends to disagree, but no one did. They appeared as worried as he felt. "Maybe I should be locked in my room, before I do something worse than I've already done."

"We've been trying to think of a way to protect you," Samuel said, pinching the stone totem of the coyote. "I'm going to call one of my spirit helpers to guard you."

"Not the coyote," Kyle protested. "It took forever to get rid of the fleas the last time it came here."

But the room was already filling with the unmistakable odor of wet fur. A dark smudge fell from the air and hit the floor with a loud plop. A coyote formed from the black puddle. It stood and shook its body, spraying the room with drops of water. Mud oozed from its paws and the tip of its tail.

"Man, he stinks," Berto said, covering his nose.

"I don't understand it," Samuel said, as if he were ashamed of the beast he had conjured. "My great-grandfather used to call forth such beautiful creatures. You'd think I'd get the same animals."

Kyle fell back against his pillows, shaking his head.

"Sorry," Samuel said, looking at the paw

prints on the floor. "I'll clean everything tomorrow. I don't know where he goes when he's not with me."

"My guess is, a swamp," Obie said and started laughing.

The coyote pricked up its ears, as if it understood that Obie was making fun of it. Its brown eyes looked as miserable as Kyle felt. He held out his hand and it padded over to the edge of the bed. Kyle scratched behind its ears.

"He's not much to look at," Samuel said softly. "But he'll guard you and make sure you stay put."

"Thanks," Kyle said and yawned. "I'm exhausted. I need to get some sleep."

The others said good night and left the room. As soon as Kyle was alone, he stripped and crawled under the covers, then buried his face in the pillows. He had enough worries as it was, and now he had to fear a power growing inside him.

N SATURDAY morning, Kyle awakened with a start. His mattress moved up and down as if someone had climbed on the bed, and then he remembered the coyote. The beast had kept him up most of the night, growling and pulling at the covers.

Kyle grabbed his pillow and threw it hard. "Get off my bed, you mangy mutt!"

A shrill cry followed, not a coyote sound at all, but a very girlish scream. He sat up, the sour taste of sleep in his mouth.

"Emily!" He pulled his blankets around his waist and moved back against the headboard.

She sat on the edge of his bed, in pink shorts and a halter top, holding the pillow, a mischievous smile on her lips. What had she seen? His bare backside, at least. His face burned with embarrassment.

"Relax," she said and tossed the pillow at him. "I have two brothers."

"If that was supposed to make me feel better, it didn't," Kyle said. "Your brothers are still in elementary school. How did you get in here anyway?"

"I didn't break in, if that's what you think," she said in a cheery voice. "Berto let me in."

"Figures," Kyle said glumly and hoped she couldn't smell his morning breath. He raked his fingers through his scruffy hair. He knew Berto well enough to know he had let her in on purpose, thinking it would be funny for her to catch Kyle sprawled out on the bed buck naked. Then he remembered Samuel's coyote and glanced around the room, hoping the coyote wasn't going to jump from a dark corner and scare Emily. But if it was still in the room, he didn't see it now.

Emily twisted around, following his gaze. "What are you looking for?"

"Nothing," Kyle said, and then he remembered how angry she had been the night before. "I'm surprised you came by."

"After that apology you left on my front porch? I couldn't resist." She smiled brightly.

He winced. He had thought he'd spent a restless night in his room, fighting the coyote for covers, but he must have had another blackout and left the apartment. Samuel's coyote was no better at being a watchdog than it was at being a power animal. With a jolt, he remembered he wasn't wearing pajamas. He hoped he'd worn something when he'd gone out.

"Kyle?" Emily said. "What's wrong with you?"

"I'm sorry, Emily. It's just . . ." How could he explain to her what was going on? "It's been a hard week. That's all."

"But it ended well," she said, her tone implying that everything that had happened the previous night was forgiven. "I love mangos and papayas. I practically ate the whole basket of fruit. But actually, it was the poem that made me change my mind about you. You're very sweet." She grabbed his toe and wiggled it.

"A poem?" he said. The last poem he remembered writing was a childish, roses-are-red verse for Mrs. Caine, one of his foster mothers.

"It was beautiful," Emily said, and her eyes took on a dreamy look.

Kyle pinched the bridge of his nose, trying to force back the memory, but as hard as he tried, he couldn't remember leaving a basket or a poem, or going anywhere near her house.

"I came over to invite you to a Christmas party at Maddie's house two weeks from today," she said.

"That sounds like fun," he said, and hoped that this time he'd remember their date. "What time should I pick you up?"

But if she had heard him, she didn't respond—something else had caught her attention. She picked up a drawing from among the dozens scattered about the floor. He must have drawn them during the night, but he couldn't remember that, either. He glanced at his fingers. No traces of charcoal or chalk lined his nails.

"Is this the kind of thing you usually draw?" Emily looked unsure. "I mean, the work is incredibly lifelike, but the subject matter is . . ." Her words fell away, and she stared at the drawing.

Kyle glanced at the picture and his stomach turned. Emily held a realistic depiction of a grisly murder, or at least that was what he thought it must be. He got out of bed, holding the covers around his waist, and picked up another page from his sketch pad. He stared at it in disbelief.

"I'd heard that your paintings were edgy," Emily said. "But I never thought they were this extreme."

She set the drawing on the bed and wiped her hands down the front of her shorts, as if holding the picture had transferred something vile to her skin. "I've got to go," she said, but she wasn't smiling. "I promised Maddie I'd meet her at the Grove for breakfast."

As soon as she left, Kyle gathered the sketches, wondering how he could have imagined such scenes. Then cold terror raced through him, and the drawings fluttered from his hands. In his blackouts before, he had done things that he wouldn't normally have done. Could he have committed the crimes the pictures portrayed?

CHAPTER FIVE

KYLE RAN INTO the front room, tripping over the tail of the sheet he held wrapped around his waist. He grabbed the remote, turned on the TV, and flipped through the channels until he found the news. If anything close to what had been shown in the drawings had happened, it would be the lead story.

But instead of a crime scene, he saw Santa Claus, waving at him. The Christmas toy drive was the big news. "Thank you," he whispered in prayer, feeling almost giddy.

"I've never seen you react so strongly to a girl." Berto walked into the room, eating strips of bacon between slices of burnt toast and tossing bites to the coyote and a huge black bear, a power animal that had just appeared one day. "What did she do to you in there?" Berto teased.

"Nothing," Kyle said, lightheartedly. "It's what didn't happen." He told Berto everything Emily had said and then took him into his room and showed him the sketches.

"Sacred offerings of human blood," Berto whispered, seeming fascinated rather than repulsed. "Man, these are like something from my era."

Kyle pulled on a robe, picked up the drawings, then took the one Berto was holding and chucked the sketches in the trash.

"You could sell those," Berto said.

"I don't want to meet the kind of people who would buy them." Kyle glanced at his bedroom clock. "Staying cooped up in here doesn't stop the blackouts, and if I hurry I can still make my audition." He started down the hallway toward the bathroom.

"Obie borrowed your car," Berto said, following after him.

"He didn't ask." Kyle stopped. "He doesn't have a driver's license."

"He figured you weren't going to be using the car today, anyway." Berto shrugged, not grasping the need for a license. "You said last night you were going to stay here, and he needed to pick up a few things for the music video they're making tonight. He won't be back for a couple of hours."

"It's all right." Kyle started down the hallway again. "I'll catch the bus."

"Let me give you a lift," Berto said.

"You can't. You pulled your bike apart." Kyle turned in to the bathroom and flipped on the lights. The bear was lapping water from the toilet.

"Trust me. I can get my bike back together before you have to leave." Berto grinned and left Kyle alone with the bear. The huge animal looked up at Kyle, uninterested, and lumbered across the tiles, his claws clicking in a slow, even rhythm.

Kyle showered, shaved, and dressed in faded jeans. He wore his tie loose and his shirt-collar button undone. At last he walked outside, eager for his audition.

Berto stood at the curb beside his Yamaha, puzzling over two screws and a long piece of metal. "These were left over." He held them in his hands for Kyle to examine.

"They must be something from the crankshaft or transmission," Kyle said. "You'll have to pull your bike apart again."

"They were probably factory-optional equipment, anyway," Berto said and tossed the parts aside. They clanked on the sidewalk. He mounted the bike with cocky assurance. "I promised I'd give you a ride."

"No way," Kyle said. "It won't start."

In answer Berto knocked the kickstand up and hit the starter button. The engine fired, and the smell of exhaust enveloped Kyle.

"I know my bike," Berto said.

"How do you have such good luck?" Kyle asked, climbing on behind him.

"It's not luck," Berto answered. "My faith is strong." Then he pushed the lever down to engage first gear and shot into the street without checking traffic.

A truck nearly clipped them, but Berto swerved away.

Kyle hoped the missing parts had nothing to do with the brakes, but he didn't worry about it for long. He was enjoying the ride too much.

They sped past Union Station into the city. Traffic snarled, and Berto took the sidewalk. The bike bounced over the curb, and when they turned down Santee Alley, dresses, shirts, and sweaters hanging outside the stalls flapped around them like brightly colored flags. Berto zigzagged around bins filled with socks and visors. Vendors yelled at him in different languages, and then the bike was airborne for a moment before they flew back onto the street. They landed with a jolt, and Berto turned left, heading for the west side.

Moments later, they parked near the off-duty police officer moonlighting as a security guard. The officer kept unauthorized visitors from wandering onto the set. Fans had already started gathering across the street, hoping for a glimpse of their favorite stars.

As soon as Kyle jumped off the bike, the production assistant ran toward him, waving her thin arms. "The casting director needs to see you right away."

"Okay," Kyle said, hoping his audition hadn't been canceled because he was late.

"How can you be so totally laid back?" she asked, tapping her fingers on her clipboard. "I mean, I'd, like, die if a big heavyweight director wanted me in his next picture."

"He wants me?" Kyle exchanged a quick glance with Berto. "My audition isn't until ten."

"Right," she said and waved him away. She ran back the way she had come, speaking into her headphone. "I found him."

"How could I have the part?" Kyle asked.

"Never question good fortune," Berto said. "Maybe they liked your look. Besides, I've been praying to Tezcatlipoca for you. You've been going through hard times, and you helped me when . . ." He stopped himself before he got emotional. His voice was hoarse when he continued. "You've always been a good friend; now I'm returning the favor."

"Thanks," Kyle said, but secretly he feared Berto's Toltec god. An aura of danger surrounded Berto whenever he lit incense and prayed to the ancient deity.

"Don't worry," Berto went on, as if he could read Kyle's thoughts. "Tezcatlipoca won't whisk you away to some dreamland. You have to be a believer for that honor."

"Good," Kyle answered and smiled.

Berto backed up his bike and then, with a rumble of tailpipes, raced away.

Kyle turned and meandered around the crew members who were laying cable and rigging lights. Then he ran up the wooden steps to the casting director's trailer and went inside without knocking.

"Kyle." Dora seemed delighted to see him. She got up from her desk, picked up a remote, and pressed PLAY. "You're incredible. The director was so impressed by your tape that he canceled the rest of the auditions. I've been waiting to show you your read-through."

Dizziness swept over Kyle as he stared at himself on the screen. It was his voice, his mannerisms, his face, but why couldn't he remember doing the scene? He slumped into a chair and groaned.

"Don't worry." Dora patted his knee. "I've seen actors vomit when they watched themselves perform. Just trust me when I tell you you're great."

"My audition wasn't until ten," Kyle said, trying to make sense of what was going on.

"I don't know how you talked the director into seeing you early. You must have hypnotized him."

"Probably," Kyle muttered.

"I was surprised to see you on the set first thing," Dora continued, as she started searching through some papers on her desk. "Four in the morning is an early call."

Kyle nodded, but he felt something closing in on him. His blackouts were apparently frequent, and he reasoned that he should feel at least some confusion of time, yet he felt none.

"Kyle?" Dora shook his arm, a worried look on her face. "Are you all right? Didn't you hear me? I said I have contracts for you to sign. I thought you'd be excited. Unless you decided to get an agent. Is that what's troubling you? We can certainly wait. Anyone would want to represent you now."

He suddenly felt too claustrophobic to remain inside. He bolted from the trailer, jumped down the stairs, and sprinted around the generators. He kept running until he was off the set and his feet were pounding down the middle of the road.

A black SUV with tinted windows was parked across the street, and as Kyle approached, a window came down. A telephoto lens was aimed at him. The editors at the tabloids must have learned that he had gotten the part in the epic film, and a photographer was already trying to capture a candid shot of him. The story wasn't going to be the one they thought they were getting, but they would like this one better: *Unknown Actor Turns Down Major Role.*

Kyle gasped, realizing how much this

moment had cost him, but he couldn't go back, even if leaving meant losing the part. He had to find out what was going on in his life.

By the time he arrived back at the loft, his shirt was drenched with sweat, and he was shivering from a growing internal cold.

Obie sat on the floor in a pool of sunlight, playing his guitar, and singing a haunting tune. He glanced up and set the guitar aside. "Are bounty hunters chasing you?"

"No." Kyle collapsed on the floor next to him. The sunshine beaming through the window warmed his back but did little to melt the fear inside him. "Cast the stones for me. I need to know what's in my future."

Obie left, then returned, carrying a leather pouch that had belonged to his mother. He joined Kyle on the floor and emptied the contents. Small gray stones clattered across the floor, each inscribed with a single letter from the runic alphabet. But, instead of reading the cast, Obie swept the stones back into his hands.

"What's wrong?" Kyle asked.

"Sometimes the cast is unclear." Obie shook the stones, but when he dropped them again, the same look of apprehension crossed his face. He started to collect the runes, but this time Kyle grabbed his wrist.

"Read what's there," Kyle said.

"You're in danger," Obie said.

"Tell me something I don't know." Kyle let out a bitter laugh. He couldn't avoid the future racing toward him, but he wanted an inkling of what was to come.

Obie scooped up the runes and held them in his cupped hands. "Draw one."

Kyle dug his fingers into the pile and pulled out a stone inscribed with a letter that looked something like a capital *H*.

"That's *hagalaz*," Obie whispered. "You can expect disruption—"

"What else is new?" Kyle asked.

"*Hagalaz* is also called the great awakener," Obie continued. "Your reality is going to change and also your understanding of yourself. We talked about your childhood once. You never found out anything about your real parents."

"No," Kyle answered, hating the sympathetic look in Obie's eyes. His roommates lived centuries from their homes, but they knew they had parents who had loved them. Kyle didn't have that comfort. He didn't know who his parents were, and from the way he had been abandoned, he doubted he'd even want to know them.

"And your childhood?" Obie probed.

"Bad memories," Kyle said. "Except for the short time I lived with Mrs. Caine." Kyle fell silent. It was hard talking about those years. The one thing he had yearned for was a sense of belonging, and that was the one thing he had never had. He'd thought he had a chance for it with Mrs. Caine, but he had been taken from her and put in another foster home. He still didn't understand why.

"It could be really important. Try to remember," Obie coaxed, his jugular vein pulsing rapidly, belying his calm tone.

"I know you're not telling me everything," Kyle said. "What is it?"

"Something from your childhood is coming

back to haunt you," Obie answered. "If we talk about those years, maybe we can figure out what it is."

"My memories are blurred," Kyle said bluntly. "I lived in too many foster homes to put them in order. In third grade I moved eleven times. That was probably the worst year. I don't think I could have survived without Mrs. Caine. She was like a real mother to me. Even after I was placed in a different home, I kept going back to visit her."

"Maybe you should go see her now," Obie encouraged.

"I doubt she even lives in the same place," Kyle answered. "I haven't gone over to the valley since I escaped from Nefandus. I was too afraid bounty hunters might follow me to her house and harm her."

"I think you have to take the risk," Obie said. "Or maybe you could call a friend from those days. Someone else might remember something that you've forgotten."

Kyle shook his head, wondering why it had been so hard for him to make friends. Other kids in foster placement had pals, but he had always been by himself.

"I really don't want to relive things." Kyle impulsively picked out two more stones and displayed them on his open palm. The first was marked with two triangles pointing at each other. The second stone had no inscription. "Just tell me what the runes say."

Obie paled. "When you draw *dagaz* and then the blank rune, the stones portend death."

"My master in Nefandus made me immortal," Kyle said. "I can't die."

Obie stared at him. "Maybe the death foretold is an extinction of your inner self, not your body. What happens if you can't come back from one of your blackouts?"

CHAPTER SIX

RS. CAINE HAD already put up her holiday decorations. Christmas lights were strung from the eaves, and a tree with tinsel and bulbs adorned the front window. Kyle stepped across the porch and started to knock, but stopped as the feeling of being watched crept across his back. He turned, but saw nothing unusual in the yard. A plastic snowman covered with dust sat on the front lawn, rocking in the breeze.

Still uneasy, he rapped on the door. He hoped Mrs. Caine was home. He'd never been able to call ahead when he came to visit, because she didn't have a phone. He assumed she couldn't afford one. She had never worked, and now that he had to pay rent and utilities, he wondered how she had managed. She had never married or had children, and he felt sorry for her, living alone. But he was grateful she hadn't moved from her house by the railroad tracks.

The door opened tentatively, and Mrs. Caine peeked out. She wore a bulky sweater, as if she were cold.

"Mrs. Caine," he said, and leaned in closer. "It's me. Kyle."

"Kyle?" The pinched lines on her face turned into a smile. She swung the door open. "Shame on you," she said, hugging him. "You stayed away too long this time."

"I'm sorry." He started to apologize, but before he could, she bustled around him and peered outside, looking both ways and finally closing and locking the door.

"Are you afraid of something?" Kyle asked, convinced that she was.

"The neighborhood," she said. "Some kids have been causing trouble."

"That's all?" he asked, watching her carefully. Her explanation didn't feel right.

"Of course, what else could it be?" She tried to laugh his concern away, but he had the growing sense that something more was making her uneasy.

He started to look out the front window, but the Christmas tree caught his attention. He leaned in toward the needles, savoring the piney scent. The candy-cane reindeer he had made in third grade decorated the branches.

"It's cozier in the kitchen," Mrs. Caine said and motioned him away from the window. "Let's go in there."

He glanced back at the living room, feeling certain she hadn't wanted him to stand where someone outside could look in and see him. He wondered if gangs were a problem. Could she have been worried about drive-by shootings?

In the hallway, he caught the unmistakable spicy scent of a man's cologne. "Mrs. Caine?" Kyle said, surprised. "Is someone living with you?"

"I thought you knew," she said and pushed through the swinging door into the kitchen. The aroma of oatmeal cookies surrounded him.

"No, but I'm glad you're no longer alone," he answered, taking his usual place at the table. "Tell me about him."

"I will not," she said and opened the refrigerator. "We're not going to talk about me. I'm concerned about you. You must have an important reason for coming all the way out here."

She pulled out a carton of milk, poured some into a glass, then lifted a warm cookie from a tray, and gave both to Kyle. She glanced up and their eyes met. "Is everything all right?"

Kyle took one bite. He was too tense to eat, so he slipped the cookie into his jacket pocket for later. "I need to know about my childhood."

The radio had been playing Christmas carols, and now Mrs. Caine switched it off. The silence filled with an edgy tension.

Mrs. Caine poured a cup of coffee, and sat across from him, clutching the mug. "I don't know much. You only lived with me a short time."

"It's important," he said, more curious now than before. "Any little detail can help me."

"I remember you embellished everything with fantasy," she said, and added a laugh, as if enjoying her memories of him. "Lots of children do, but you were a little old to be doing it still."

"I don't remember that," Kyle answered honestly. "I made up stories?"

She nodded. "It got you into quite a bit of trouble."

He tried to remember. He had been sent to the principal's office frequently for doing things he hadn't done. At the time he had felt picked on and thought his classmates were lying to get him in trouble, but maybe he had been having blackouts even then. "What else?"

"Are you sure you want to hear?" she said. "Maybe some things are better left in the past."

He didn't know what she was referring to. "It's important." He leaned closer, anxious to listen.

"You were only eight years old when you came to live with me, but the county had already sealed your records."

He clasped the edge of the table as his

mind rushed back to the drawings Emily had found scattered about his room. "Court records are sealed for minors only when they've committed some atrocity," he said. "What did I do?"

"Records can be sealed for any number of reasons," she explained. "Maybe you stole something. Goodness knows you had good reason. When you arrived here you were skin and bones, with hardly anything to wear."

"You don't know why they were sealed?" he asked.

"It's normal in the juvenile court system not to leave the trial court records open."

"Trial? I don't remember going to court. I would remember something as important as that."

"There were never any criminal proceedings that I know about. The government took the county to court," she said, shrugging. "They wanted your case history sealed."

"But that's confidential anyway," he said, wondering what could have been in his records. "No one could have access to it."

"They didn't want the social workers to read—" she stopped.

"What?" he asked impatiently.

"About you," she answered mysteriously.

"What about me?" he asked.

She shrugged. "No one ever told me."

He stared at her, positive she knew and wasn't saying. Was there violence buried in his past? Maybe that part of him was reawakening now. Before he could ask more, a terrible premonition came over him. He looked up for reassurance from Mrs. Caine, but instead of seeing her nurturing smile, he saw tight lines appear around her mouth as if she were worried. Her fingers fidgeted with the mug. Was she afraid of the danger looming inside him, too? Perhaps she feared what he was capable of becoming. He believed she knew more than she was saying, but what was she holding back?

He stood abruptly, knocking his chair over and causing the milk in his glass to slosh over the side.

"Kyle?" Mrs. Caine asked. "Are you all right?"

"I have to leave," he answered, an irrational fear seizing him. He could never harm Mrs. Caine, could he? He wouldn't hurt someone he loved as deeply as he loved her, but until he understood his blackouts, he couldn't trust himself completely, either.

"It's not you I'm afraid of," Mrs. Caine said, as if she could read his thoughts.

"Maybe you should be," he answered. "Lock the door after me, and don't let me back in."

CHAPTER SEVEN

IRLS IN SPIKED heels and short skirts crowded the sidewalk, waiting in line at the open casting call for the music video of Obie's band. A choreographer stood in the street, teaching one group the dance steps for the audition.

Kyle watched briefly and then, ignoring the security guard, entered the sound studio. A disheartening weariness had settled over him, and he felt embarrassed by his earlier behavior. He wished Mrs. Caine had a phone, so he could have called her and apologized for leaving as abruptly as he had.

He walked through a dark hall and peered

into the room where Obie stood in the center of a false cityscape with the other band members, Les, Nolo, and Dacey.

A girl sprayed water over Obie's face and across his T-shirt. He looked up, annoyed. Then he saw Kyle and waved him on to the set.

"She says I have to look sweaty and gross, like I've been singing for hours, but the director won't let me play my guitar," Obie complained. "You'd think they'd want the real stuff."

"That's Hollywood." Kyle shrugged.

A young director hurried over to Obie, lighting a cigarette. "Can you dangle this in your mouth?"

"Why?" Obie asked, waving the smoke away from his face.

"The pose projects danger," the director explained.

"Smoking makes me look dangerous?" Obie gave the director a contemptuous look, then threw his head back and let out his battle cry. Kyle had heard the scream before and covered his ears. Visigoth warriors had made the sound to frighten their enemies when they charged into battle.

The director stepped back, his face ashen, and tossed the cigarette aside.

Les, Nolo, and Dacey laughed.

"Get a close-up when he does his scream," the director said to the cameraman, and he hurried back to his monitor. "I mean, go down his throat."

"Can we get on with it?" Les looked close to walking out. "I thought it was supposed to be fun. Why are the girls outside? I want to watch them dance."

"How long do we have to stand here while they fix the lights?" Dacey asked. He was sweating, and Kyle didn't think his perspiration came from a spray bottle.

"This sucks," Nolo said, twirling the drumsticks between his fingers as if his hands were impatient to mark out the beat. "I thought they'd let us play."

"How are they going to stop us?" Obie plugged in, and then Les and Dacey did the same.

"Rock and roll!" Les screamed, and threw a fist in the air, then brought his hand down hard and strummed the first chord.

Obie and Dacey broke into song, and Kyle hurried out of the camera's way. He scanned the crowd standing behind the equipment. Samuel and Berto were leaning against the wall. He joined them.

Berto started to say something, but the music was loud and soaring. He motioned for the other two to follow him outside. Soon, they stood on the curb, watching the girls behind the choreographer rotate their hips. The dancers turned in unison, their footsteps making a clapping sound against the pavement.

Berto spoke first. "I saw you with Ashley this afternoon."

"That's impossible," Kyle answered. "I was with Mrs. Caine. Obie should have told you I was going to visit her."

"He did." Samuel nodded. "We knew where you were supposed to be."

"You don't believe me?" Kyle asked, surprised.

"I saw you with Ashley," Berto repeated, his stance daring Kyle to contradict him.

Kyle glared at Berto, wondering why he would lie, but just as quickly another thought occurred to him. "What were you doing at Ashley's place?"

"It wasn't like I was visiting her," Berto said. "I sent my spirit out to see how she was doing."

Kyle's eyes locked with Berto's, and in that moment more passed between them than could be explained in words. In admitting he had seen Kyle with Ashley, Berto was revealing the depth of his love for her, but also his inability to let her go.

"I wasn't there to spy on you," Berto whispered so Samuel couldn't hear. "I go there because I can't stop myself, all right? I need to see her, and I don't have control over it." Berto looked away, clearly ashamed of his obsession.

"If I was with her," Kyle said at last, the fight gone from his voice now, "I don't remember. What I do remember is spending time with Mrs. Caine."

"Maybe Ashley's doing something to you," Samuel said, turning away from the dancers and breaking back into the conversation. "Like giving you a posthypnotic suggestion that makes you believe you were doing something other than spending time with her."

"I suppose that's possible," Kyle said. "But what would she want with me?"

"The black diamond," Samuel answered.

"I don't have it," Kyle answered. "I would remember something that important."

"I saw you showing it to her," Berto said.

"How would you even know it *was* the black diamond?" Kyle asked. "None of us have ever seen it before."

"There's no mistaking it," Berto said, and a look of awe crossed his face. "The jewel you held in your hand was so red it appeared black, and when it caught the light it looked like the sun."

"I wasn't with her." Kyle sighed heavily, and then added, "As far as I can remember."

"We believe you're telling the truth," Samuel said, "as you know the truth. But what reason would Berto have to lie? Ashley must be doing something to you."

Kyle nodded and stared at the dancers. Of the forty or more girls practicing the steps, one waved. He smiled. Emily was trying to follow the quick movements of the choreographer. She blushed, seeming shy and self-conscious. At any other time, he would have enjoyed watching the way her body moved in her pink shorts and halter top, but right now he had to concentrate on everything Samuel and Berto had told him.

First his roommates had convinced him that his emerging power was causing him to have blackouts, saying they feared it was trying to take over his personality. Now, on Berto's word alone, they had apparently decided that Ashley was controlling him and giving him some magical version of a posthypnotic suggestion, so that he wouldn't remember the time he'd spent with her. Neither explanation felt right to him.

Then he remembered the cookie in his pocket. He pulled it out and held it up. He had no doubt now that he had been with Mrs. Caine. He studied Berto. Maybe he was lying. Could he be? Was it possible that Berto had aligned himself with Ashley again?

"I was definitely at Mrs. Caine's house," Kyle said slowly, challenging Berto. "This cookie proves it."

Samuel and Berto exchanged quick looks, as if they thought Kyle were slipping over the edge.

"What does the cookie prove?" Samuel asked.

"Mrs. Caine was baking cookies," Kyle said. "So maybe Berto is lying to protect something he and Ashley are planning, and they're using me as a decoy."

Berto kept his chin high, his eyes threatening.

Kyle took a step closer.

Samuel dodged between them. "We're not going to solve anything by fighting each other. We need to use our energy to find out what's going on."

"We can go back to the apartment, and you

can search my room for the diamond," Kyle said. But then he caught Berto's guilty look, and knew they already had. "You didn't find it, did you?"

"We need the black diamond," Samuel answered. "You would have done the same if it had been one of us."

Kyle nodded, but he wasn't convinced he would have betrayed their trust.

When Obie finished performing in the music video, Kyle drove his roommates back to the loft. He would have preferred to go out with Emily, but she had said she wanted to stay and practice the routine. At last he parked and let the others go inside ahead of him. He thought about driving around the city. He wasn't in the mood to spend time with his roommates, but part of him was worried he might have another blackout. Until he understood what was happening to him, he knew it was safer for him to stay in the loft.

Finally, he left the car and went in to the apartment, but when he stepped into the front room, he found the others standing in a half circle, looking down. At first he thought they must have discovered the coyote or the bear sprawled out dead, by the way they were staring at the floor. Then he saw the torn canvas. His self-portrait had been slashed. He turned to Berto, assuming he had done it in a jealous rage after seeing Kyle with Ashley, but Berto looked as stunned as Kyle felt.

"Did your bear do this?" Kyle asked Samuel, feeling his heart sink. He had spent hours on the portrait and had planned to enter it in a citywide competition at the Museum of Contemporary Art.

"Of course not," Samuel answered. "The bear's too lazy, and the coyote would have left tooth marks on the frame."

Obie picked up the shredded canvas and examined the jagged edges. When he was finished, he glanced at Kyle, as if assessing his mental stability. "From the way it's puckered around the edges of the frame, I think someone tore it by punching their fist through it. Whoever did this must have been in a frenzy. Did you have a blackout recently?"

"Me?" Kyle answered. "Are you saying I did it?"

"No." Berto clasped Kyle's shoulder. "Not as you are right now, you wouldn't have, but—"

"But you think I did," Kyle challenged.

"We're going to help you through this," Berto said. "Whatever it is."

"I don't need anyone's help," Kyle answered, yanking away from Berto. But then he softened, as he figured out what to do. "I'm going to talk to Ashley. If what you say is true, then she's the key to what's going on."

"That's the wrong move," Samuel said. "If you really don't have a memory of the time you've been spending with her, then she must be using some kind of mind-altering magic on you. If she thinks you're suspicious of her, she could do something even worse to you."

"Obie can give me a counter-spell," Kyle said, determined to go through with his plan.

"My magic doesn't work against hers," Obie answered. "She's too strong."

"I'm willing to take the risk," Kyle said. "At least, if I make the date to see her and don't remember it afterward I'll know she's doing something to make me forget."

"Until we know more," Samuel said, "it's too dangerous."

"You're right," Kyle lied, too tired to argue more. "It's too risky." But already he was making plans to call Ashley. He didn't see that he had a choice. He couldn't continue this way.

CHAPTER EIGHT

LATE MONDAY afternoon, Kyle sat at a small table in the far corner of Sweet Lady Jane's. He tilted the French press and poured himself a cup of coffee. He hadn't slept the night before and needed a wake-up jolt of caffeine. He drank the strong brew, relishing the bitter taste, and glanced up as Ashley stepped past the front window. He switched on the tape recorder hidden in his pocket, then stood and pushed through the customers crowding the counter. He hadn't told his roommates he was meeting Ashley, but he didn't think it likely they would drop in there for tea and cake.

Ashley walked inside, her posture radiating

confidence. Christmas tinsel clung to her hair and shoulders, as if she had just come from a party. She had confided to Kyle once, tipsy after a single beer, that she had been a priestess in her own time back in Mesopotamia, and, before she had been abducted and taken to Nefandus, she had stolen the Tablet of Destinies. Kyle hadn't known what she was talking about until he had looked it up on the Internet. According to Babylonian tradition, the tablet gave absolute power to its possessor, but Kyle had wondered why the tablet hadn't protected her from her kidnappers. Ashley had desperately needed his help to return to her own time before others discovered where she had hidden the tablet. Kyle had suggested that they journey to the place where the tablet was hidden (in a part of what is now known as Iraq) and excavate it. But in response Ashley had stared at him as if he were simpleminded and hadn't understood a word she had said.

"You look lost in thought," Ashley teased, letting her fingers intertwine with his. She kissed him, and the touch of her lips made him want more. How long had it been since he'd kissed a girl without harming her? He returned her embrace, breathing in her intoxicating fragrance and loving the feel of her body against him.

"Can I help you?" a voice interrupted. The waiter behind the counter looked pointedly at the growing line, and then he lowered his eyebrows in an impatient scowl.

"It's hard to decide," Ashley said, tilting her head. She gave the waiter a flirtatious smile that made him back away from his attitude.

"What will it be?" he asked, sweetly this time.

Kyle had seen Ashley's effect on other people before. Still, it amazed him. Was it just her beauty that let her get away with things, or had she cast a spell?

"We'll each have a piece of the princess cake," Ashley said, and then she grabbed Kyle's wrist. "Why aren't you wearing the bracelet I gave you?"

He stared at her, not sure how to answer. He didn't recall receiving a gift from her, especially not a bracelet, and if he had, he didn't know what he had done with it. "I didn't want to get it wet," he lied, pulling her back to his table. "I took it off when I showered and forgot to put it back on."

"I picked it out especially for you," she said and sat on the bench beside him instead of taking the chair on the opposite side of the table. "Don't forget to wear it next time."

"I promise," he said and poured a cup of coffee for her. If Ashley were controlling his mind, as his roommates suspected, then why would she give him something tangible, like a bracelet, that when he returned to his normal awareness would make him question where he had been?

"Did you bring the black diamond?" she whispered and brazenly spread her fingers over the outside of his jeans pockets, searching.

"I don't have it," he answered, moving her hands, fearful she'd discover the tape recorder.

"I thought you were going to let me hold the diamond." She ended her sentence by touching his chin and turning his head to face her. Her lips parted, waiting. He kissed her, even though he knew he shouldn't.

"Excuse me," the waiter interrupted.

Kyle slowly pulled away from Ashley.

The waiter set two plates on the marble tabletop. "I'm rather enjoying your romantic display," he said, "but I think some of our customers disapprove."

Kyle followed the waiter's glance. At the end of the counter, near the cash register, Emily and Maddie stood, staring back at them. Emily looked as if she were ready to burst into tears.

"Damn," Kyle muttered, and shot up, jarring the table and spilling the coffee.

"My dress," Ashley yelled, grabbing a napkin.

Kyle knew he needed to stay with Ashley, but he couldn't bear the hurt look on Emily's face.

"I warned you," Maddie said to Emily as Kyle approached. "Samuel tried to stick up for Kyle, but I knew he was fooling around. This is living proof."

"It's not what you think," Kyle said in a low voice. He tried to take Emily's hand. "I can explain."

"You don't owe me an explanation," Emily said coldly. "It's not like I thought we were going out." But her expression belied her words. He could see the misery in her eyes.

"Ashley is just . . ." He started to say *a friend*, but he caught Ashley's reflection in the mirror that ran the length of the pastry shop, and reality set in. He couldn't afford to offend Ashley. His life might literally depend on keeping her his ally.

"What's going on?" Ashley said peevishly as she approached them, still wiping at the coffee stain.

"Kyle, you're such a jerk," Maddie said angrily. "How can you treat Emily this way? You know what she's been through."

"I'm sorry," Kyle said.

Ashley fumed. "Why are you apologizing to her? You should be apologizing to me. Look at my dress."

"I'll buy you a new one," Kyle said,

knowing he couldn't; her one outfit must have cost more than his car was worth; then, to Emily, he said, "It's not what it seems. Trust me."

Emily stared at Kyle, unsure, but Maddie rolled her eyes. "Are you for real?" She seized Emily's arm and guided her toward the door.

Kyle turned back to Ashley and held his hands up in a pleading gesture, trying to stop her anger. "I have to take care of this. Just wait here. I'll be right back." He turned and followed Emily and Maddie outside.

"Let me explain," he said when he reached Maddie's car.

Emily wiped her eyes, but mascara stains had already given her a raccoon look.

"I . . ." he stuttered. He had no idea what he would say. Would Emily even believe him if he did tell her the truth?

"You'd better explain to me first," Ashley said from behind him.

Kyle spun around. "Can't you ever do anything anyone asks you to do? I told you I'd be right back."

"This is more interesting," Ashley said, her eyes fiery.

Maddie smirked. "I guess you finally got caught at your own game." She unlocked the door to her huge car. The back bumper was badly dented, as if she often took out her frustrations on whatever happened to be parked behind her.

Emily climbed in as Maddie ran around to the driver's side. She fumbled with her keys, then slid in behind the steering wheel. The large crucifix hanging from her rearview mirror swayed as she gunned the engine.

Black smoke churned around Kyle and his shoulders slumped hopelessly. "Maddie, please."

The car took off, rattling loudly, the rainbow letters on the back window flashing *Chicks Rule*.

Kyle turned, defeated, and stared at Ashley, trying to think of something—anything—to explain his behavior. "Ashley, please understand," he said, hoping she'd believe his lie. "Emily's been crushing on me, and you know she's been through a lot. I didn't want to hurt her feelings."

"Like I care," Ashley said. The firestorm in her eyes hadn't settled yet.

"I'll give you the black diamond," he said, knowing he couldn't deliver, and he pulled her to him. "You care about that."

"Do you promise this time?" she asked, softening.

"I promise," he said, and cupped her face in his hands; then he kissed her. She returned his embrace. He hated himself for what he was doing. He didn't have the diamond, and what was she going to do when she found out? But he couldn't worry about that now. He needed to get as much information from her as he could before she uncovered his scheme.

A car horn blasted, startling him. Kyle looked up as Maddie's car sped by. Emily looked out the window and waved him off with a not-so-friendly hand gesture.

"Damn," he whispered. "Maddie must have circled the block to prove her point to Emily."

"What do you care?" Ashley asked dreamily, but then she gazed into his eyes and caught his troubled look. She stomped away from him, livid, and placed her hands on her hips. "Maddie's right about one thing. You're a loser, Kyle."

"She didn't say that," Kyle said.

"She should have." Ashley grinned, then turned and walked into the entrance of an antique shop.

"Ashley." Kyle ran after her. "You can't, not here."

"I'm never second best," she warned, tossing her hair. "Always remember that, Kyle. I'm never second."

"Don't," he said, knowing what she was going to do. "Someone will see you."

"Like I care," she answered, and dematerialized into a plume of smoky air.

"Great." Kyle sighed heavily, beaten; then he squinted and coughed as the shadow streamed over his face and ruffled his hair. He watched the dark cloud sail away and wondered if Ashley was going home or back to Nefandus.

He needed to leave, in case she returned with a posse of Regulators.

He started down Melrose, the winter shadows long and stretching ahead of him. He didn't know how his life could become any more messed up than it was.

He crossed the next street, and a curious feeling made him pause and look back. The winter sun hovered near the horizon, its white glare blinding him, but nothing seemed out of the ordinary. Even so his hands began shaking uncontrollably and sweat gathered on his forehead. He wondered if this could be the physical prelude to one of his blackouts. He took three more steps and stopped in front of a liquor store, feeling as if he were going to pass out. Then he caught a glimpse of himself in the window and flinched. He was standing perfectly still, but in the glass his reflection kept walking toward him. Dumbfounded, he turned sharply, almost losing his balance, and stared at a person who looked exactly like him.

"Don't you remember me?" his double said, nonchalantly tearing open a bag of potato chips.

CHAPTER NINE

KYLE PRESSED against the plate-glass
window behind him, trying to put more distance
between himself and the hallucination walking
toward him. He sensed he was being sucked
down into a world of his own imagining, a wak-
ing nightmare from which he might never
return.

"Kylie-Kyle-Kyle," the double said, in the
childish, singsong manner that Kyle remembered so well. The voice had terrified him as a
child, and now the same cold terror made his
stomach turn.

"I'm your twin brother, Kent. I'm real,"
Kent said, reading Kyle's mind. "Touch me."

He held out his hand, but Kyle shied away, pushing back hard and making the window vibrate perilously.

"They brainwashed you." Kent stuffed a handful of potato chips into his mouth. "Even so, I thought seeing me might spark a memory or two."

"They told me you weren't real," Kyle ventured at last, trying to steady his breathing. "Doc Witherspoon said my loneliness made me create an imaginary twin. Everyone assured me that I didn't have a brother."

"They told *me* you had abandoned me," Kent answered.

"How could I abandon you?" Kyle asked and stepped away from the window. "I was only a kid. I couldn't control where I was sent to live."

"Why'd you let them convince you that I was only a figment of your imagination?" Kent asked, and anger seemed to rise off him in waves. "I'm your flesh and blood. The only kin you have."

Kyle guiltily considered what Kent said, but

it only brought forth a question of his own. "Why would they want to separate us?"

"You tell me."

"I don't know," Kyle answered. "It doesn't make sense; even if they couldn't place two brothers in one home, they wouldn't need to lie. Lots of families are split apart, but the kids aren't told their siblings don't exist."

"They couldn't dissuade me," Kent said proudly. "I always knew you were real and out there somewhere, waiting for me."

"But why would they lie to me?" Kyle asked, wondering if Mrs. Caine had also known. Could she have kept the truth from him, too? Then he turned his attention back to Kent. "But if you knew I existed, why didn't you try to find me sooner?"

"How would I know you wanted to see me?" Kent asked. "You betrayed me. You told everyone you didn't have a family."

Kyle tried to steady himself, astounded by the rapid change in his own emotions, but he also felt an overwhelming sense of relief. "I haven't been having memory lapses, have I?"

His mind raced through the past weeks. "And no one hexed me or gave me a posthypnotic suggestion. It was you all along. You did the things that got me into trouble."

"Why do you always look at the bad side?" Kent complained. "You're such a buzz-kill. You should be grateful for all the good I've done for you."

"Like what?" Kyle asked, baffled.

"I hooked you up with Emily, for one thing," Kent answered. "Do you think she started crushing on you for no reason? I flirted with her, pretending I was you, and got her interested, but you keep destroying all my hard work. I had to apologize for your bad behavior with a basket of fruit and a poem, and now I just watched you mess it up again. What were you doing with Ashley, anyway? She's mine even though she thinks I'm you. That will change when I'm ready to tell her I'm your twin."

Kent's revelation made another piece of the mystery fall into place. "Berto saw her with *you*," Kyle said. "That means you have the black diamond."

"Where is your gratitude?" Kent ignored Kyle's comment and blustered on. "It was my read-through that got you the costarring role. You blew that, too. What is it with you, some bleak, self-fulfilling prophecy? Can't you enjoy life? Where's your joy?"

"I have fun," Kyle protested.

"I thought when I fiddled with your painting you'd get the idea that spending time alone in front of a canvas isn't what you're supposed to do." He flung the bag of potato chips aside, scattering chips across the sidewalk. "You need to be out living life."

"You destroyed my self-portrait," Kyle said angrily.

"You should be thanking me," Kent answered.

"What are you saying?" Kyle asked.

"I'm saying you're an idiot for wasting your life the way you are; what do you think I'm saying?"

Kyle started to answer, but he caught a glint of silver and stared at the bracelet that looked like a coil of barbed wire wrapped around Kent's wrist. He felt certain it was the bracelet Ashley had been talking about.

"I can't believe you're going to pout about your painting," Kent said, misreading Kyle's silence. "I gave you enough sketches beforehand to compensate you. You should have sold them."

"They were disgusting," Kyle said.

Distant sirens filled the air, and Kent started walking toward Kyle's car. "You've always been such doom and gloom," Kent added. "Even when we were little, you wouldn't play with the other kids, because you were afraid of hurting them. So I had to beat them up for you."

"You're the reason I was in the principal's office all the time," Kyle said, following Kent. "But why did the teachers blame me? They must have known you did it." His brain felt jammed with all the new information, and he stared at Kent, hoping he'd explain.

"You promised to protect me," Kent said simply, and he stopped at the curb next to Kyle's car.

"That's why I took the punishment for you?" Kyle asked. "Because I promised to protect you?"

"That's what brothers do," Kent said.

A hollowness filled Kyle's chest. How had he let Doc Witherspoon convince him that he didn't have a brother? He had failed Kent.

"I don't care about the past," Kyle said, suddenly overcome with gratitude that his brother was with him again. He wanted to build a new relationship with Kent. "I'm grateful we're finally reunited." He embraced his brother, but the strong aroma of Kent's aftershave made him pull back. "You've got to do something about that killer cologne," he said, taking on the big-brother role and enjoying it. "C'mon, I want you to meet my roommates." He took the car keys from his pocket.

Kent frowned. "I'm not here for a family reunion."

Something in the way he said it made Kyle uneasy. "What's up?"

"I got in a little trouble this afternoon," Kent went on. "Not my fault, really. If you'd put more money in the box I wouldn't have been forced to steal from outside."

"You took the money I put in?" Kyle said, but his thoughts had fast-forwarded; Kent had done everything for which Kyle had been accused, including stealing the money for the rent and utilities. "What did you do to get in trouble?"

"I just swiped the bag of chips," Kent said. "Who would have thought the owner of the minimart would have made such a fuss?"

"What happened?" Kyle knew intuitively that Kent had done something worse than steal a bag of potato chips, and, as if in answer, the sirens grew louder.

Kent looked back down the street, his muscles tensing.

"Running will make it worse," Kyle offered, understanding why Kent appeared so anxious to get into the car. "You have to face up to what you've done. I'll drive you back to the minimart, and you can apologize."

He put a brotherly arm around Kent's shoulder, but as he leaned forward to unlock the passenger-side door, he stopped and turned back. He stood close enough to feel Kent's breath, and yet he felt none. In disbelief, Kyle lifted his hand, fingers splayed in front of Kent's face. His chest moved up and down, expanding and contracting like a bellows, but without drawing or expelling air.

"What are you?" Kyle asked. "You don't breathe."

"I will soon enough." Kent ripped the car keys from Kyle's hand and raced around the Impala to the driver's side.

"Wait." Kyle ran after him, determined to stop him.

But Kent spun around and punched Kyle, knocking him down to the pavement, then he jumped into the car, gunned the engine, and backed up. Kyle rolled away from the tires.

"See ya, bro," Kent yelled, his reflection in the side-view mirror grinning down at Kyle.

As the car sped away, Kyle caught a lingering whiff of Kent's cologne and suddenly remembered where he had smelled the fragrance before. As he stood, an LAPD squad car turned the corner coming off La Cienega, its lights flashing.

Kyle hesitated, considering his options. Would the officers even believe him if he told them Kent had committed the crime? He couldn't allow himself to be captured. He sensed that Kent was a danger to more people than just himself, and right now he was the only one who knew about Kent's existence.

As the police car screeched to a stop, Kyle dodged into oncoming traffic and sprinted across the street. He dashed around a line of trash cans and raced into a narrow opening between two buildings, but when he reached the back, the brick walls from adjoining stores trapped him in a dead end. He stared at three rusted doors, unsure which one to try.

Footsteps pounded behind him, and then the air overhead filled with the thundering vibration of a police helicopter. He opened the first door, closing it behind him, and stumbled into the dark. The smells of urine and mildew stung his nose.

His eyes hadn't yet adjusted to the gloom

when he heard the doorknob turn. He had no choice. He had to become a shadow in order to escape.

A police officer opened the door. Handcuffs clattered as he unhooked them from his utility belt. "Come out with your hands clasped behind your head."

Kyle willed his jittery body to relax, but he was shaking so badly he could feel the cartons behind him begin to move. He dematerialized bit by bit, turning into splotches of flesh and churning specks before fading into an inky blur.

The policeman stepped back, fear flashing in his eyes as the handcuffs slipped from his fingers and clattered on the concrete. He fumbled with his holster and drew his gun.

Kyle panicked and tried to reassure the officer that he meant no harm, but when he spoke, his words stretched eerily through his thin vocal cords and came out in a haunting shriek.

The officer fired repeatedly. Shot after shot exploded in the small storage room. The blasts echoed through Kyle and made him ricochet against the walls. His body changed and changed back, flashing between ghost and solid form. He was swept up to the ceiling, a phantom, and began materializing on the way. He whacked his head hard against a light fixture. Plaster was still raining down on the officer as Kyle started to fall. He caught himself in midair, and his body burst apart, rising again like a black steam. He had never dissolved so rapidly, and burning pain seared through him. His strength had left him, and he suddenly remembered stories of *servi* who had depleted their energies and had been unable to turn back to solid form again.

The officer aimed, and Kyle wondered what would happen to him if the bullet were to go through him.

CHAPTER TEN

"**W**HAT IS IT?" The second officer rounded the corner, pointing the barrel of his gun and searching for a target.

"Do you believe in ghosts?" the first officer asked.

While they were talking, Kyle stole outside, a fragment of black clinging to the darkness along the wall. With all his strength he tried to rise, but he bobbled instead, and his spectral shadow fell on top of the second officer's head. The man let out a startled cry, and his gun went off, but this time the wind caught Kyle, lifting him up and over the buildings.

He sailed toward downtown, the winter

moon rising behind gossamer veils of haze. His vision was panoramic now, and he tried to enjoy the beauty of the L.A. skyline shrouded in silver mists, but anxiety made him start to take physical form, and if anyone on the streets below had looked up, he feared they would have seen his outline, imprisoned in the wispy clouds.

By the time he reached Chinatown, he had regained some of his composure. He curled with the fog around the street lamps and let the ocean damp seep through him before he twirled into a Christmas-tree lot and became whole, the taste of evergreen lingering on his tongue.

He walked back to the loft, lost in thought, as holiday shoppers bustled around him. He had violated his own rule by disappearing in front of witnesses. He didn't know what the repercussions would be, but he hoped the officers would begin to doubt what they had seen. Kyle had to tell his roommates what had happened, but that wasn't the worst thing he had to confess.

He stepped through the front door and

stopped. Take-out cartons lay toppled across the floor. The coyote stood in the middle of the spilled food, licking at some noodles. It lifted its head and growled at Kyle, seeming to fear he might take away its chow mein. Obie and Samuel sat on pillows, eating with chopsticks, ignoring the mess, and watching an old sitcom on TV.

"Where's Berto?" Kyle asked as he stepped into the room. He wanted to tell all three roommates at one time.

But instead of answering, Obie threw his egg roll aside. He wrote a line of symbols across the air and jumped up, then flung his hand out and threw the inscription at Kyle.

"Why'd you do that?" Kyle ducked, but the incantation caught him and glowed briefly before burrowing into his skin. A warm calm filled him, and the tension in his back eased. Only then did he realize how chilled and weak he had become.

"You looked like you were ready to collapse," Obie answered, his fingers poised to cast another spell. "That was a charm to soothe. My mother used it on me all the time when I was growing up."

"What happened to you?" Samuel asked, turning off the TV. He stood and joined them, offering Kyle his carton of kung pao chicken.

Kyle ignored the food and pulled the tape recorder from his pocket. "You never answered my first question. Where's Berto?"

"He's working at Quake tonight," Samuel explained. "They wanted him at the door for a big celebrity party, to make sure no one sneaks in with a camera."

Kyle rewound the tape in his recorder, then set it on the table next to his sketches and pressed PLAY. "I wanted to tell all of you at once, but this can't wait until Berto gets back."

Obie and Samuel listened to the voices on the tape, without uttering a word.

When the recording finished, Obie spoke first. "Why were you talking to yourself?"

"Didn't you listen?" Kyle asked impatiently.

"People talk to themselves, and some-times—" Samuel began.

"But they don't answer their own

questions." Kyle sat down in the beanbag chair, too fatigued to stand any longer. "I was never kidnapped like the rest of you and taken into Nefandus," he confessed at last. "I lied. I went there freely."

"You wanted to become a Follower, a resident?" Samuel.

"No," Kyle answered. "That wasn't the reason I snuck in."

"But how did you get in?" Obie asked, not bothering to hide his doubt. "I know how to go into Nefandus because my master taught me, but most residents have to use the portals, and even then it's not easy."

"I followed a friend," Kyle answered. "He didn't know I was tagging along." But even as he spoke, Kyle wondered if that were true. Maybe Kent had set a trap.

"Did you see him once you were in Nefandus?" Samuel asked.

"Of course he couldn't have," Obie answered. "Kyle was an outsider then, so he would have seen only the mist."

The churning vapors were a barrier, in case

someone from the earth realm stumbled into Nefandus; anyone who didn't belong saw fog and clouds, not the cities and the artificial sky.

"Regulators captured me once I was inside," Kyle went on, a queasy feeling rising inside him. "But until now I never told anyone about the person I followed, because I didn't think anyone would believe me."

"We believe you," Obie said encouragingly.

"When I was young I thought I had a twin brother named Kent," Kyle said. "That's the person I followed into Nefandus. Today I saw him again. He's the guy you heard on the tape."

"Why didn't you bring him home?" Samuel asked. "He's kin."

"Didn't you hear the conversation?" Kyle asked incredulously. "Besides, even if he hadn't been running from the cops, I don't know if it would have been wise to bring him here, because I don't think he's real, not like you and me, anyway."

"You'd better tell us everything," Obie said, "starting with your first memories."

By the time Kyle had finished telling them about his childhood, it was almost midnight, and empty pizza boxes had been added to the clutter on the floor.

"I think you really do have a twin, and the two of you were separated at birth," Obie said.

"I thought the same when I saw Kent today," Kyle said. "But he wasn't breathing. He's not alive in the ordinary sense."

"You have to be mistaken," Samuel argued. "How could he exist without air? You said you were stressed; maybe he was holding his breath, teasing you. Whatever the reason, it makes more sense that you actually have a twin and that, for whatever reason, authorities wanted to keep you apart."

"His chest was moving like yours or mine," Kyle explained again. "But when I held my hand in front of his face, I couldn't feel his breath; no air came from his lungs. You heard the tape. I confronted him. I said, 'You don't breathe,' and he told me that he would soon enough."

Samuel grabbed the tape recorder, rewound the cassette, and played the last bit of the conversation again. When it finished, he stared at Kyle. "I'm not convinced he isn't your twin, but if he is some kind of clone, some entity that looks like you, then I'm assuming he led you into Nefandus on purpose; he knew you were following him, and he was hoping you'd be captured and imprisoned there for centuries, like the rest of us."

Kyle nodded his agreement.

"He wanted you out of the way," Obie continued. "And when that didn't work, he led us into Nefandus, to retrieve the black diamond."

"So he could use its wish-granting power to get rid of me," Kyle finished. "That's what I think, anyway."

"Maybe he has bigger plans," Obie said.

"In either case, he must have some kind of telepathic connection to Kyle," Samuel added. "That's the only way he could be doing everything he's done lately without coming face to face with Kyle."

"That creeps me out," Kyle said, hating the notion that Kent might be picking up his thoughts. "But I think you're right."

"The first thing we need to do is figure out what he is," Obie said. "How are we going to do that?"

"I'm sure the cologne he was wearing is the same one I smelled inside Mrs. Caine's house," Kyle said.

"You think Kent is living with your foster mom?" Samuel asked, surprised.

"I don't know, but I want to go back there and find out. Maybe there's something she's not telling me." Kyle glanced at the clock. "It's too late to visit her tonight."

"I'll go with you first thing in the morning," Obie offered. "I'll work a truth spell on her."

"Thanks." Kyle nodded, but he couldn't shake a feeling of impending doom.

CHAPTER ELEVEN

THE NEXT MORNING, Kyle and Obie ditched school and drove over the Santa Monica Mountains to the San Fernando Valley. The sprawling suburbs, endless strips malls, and morning heat depressed Kyle. He liked the energy in downtown L.A. better.

Obie slouched in the passenger seat next to him, wearing a baseball cap pulled down over his eyes. The last time he had come over the hill, Valley girls had mobbed him after a performance. This morning he was tired and in a funk, because they had left before he'd had a chance to eat.

"We'll get breakfast on the way back,"

Kyle said, trying to get Obie out of his mood. He parked the car in front of Mrs. Caine's house, and they started up the walk.

"Are railroad tracks usually so close to a house?" Obie asked as they reached the porch.

Kyle glanced at the berm. He remembered the clicking metal wheels and the chugging locomotives. The vibrations had made his bed jiggle away from the wall. "Maybe the house was built before the codes got strict," Kyle said, and rang the doorbell. He did find it odd that the roadbed for the rails almost touched the house.

Mrs. Caine opened the door. "Kyle, I knew you'd come back."

"I'm sorry about the way I ran out on you last time," he said.

"No apology necessary." She gave him a hug, then motioned him inside. "Come in. I was just having my morning coffee."

Kyle started into the house, surprised that Mrs. Caine wasn't more concerned about his brusque departure on his last visit. "This is my friend Obie," he said as he closed the front door.

"Welcome." Mrs. Caine sat down on the couch and began pouring coffee into three cups. The rich aroma filled the room.

Kyle started to take a seat but Obie grabbed his arm and kept him at the door.

"Don't you think it's odd she had three cups out already?" Obie whispered. Then, without waiting for Kyle to answer, he continued, "I mean it's really peculiar in here. I'm not from this time period, but doesn't she seem a little retro?"

Kyle glanced at the maple furniture, the plaid couch and chairs. The room looked exactly as he remembered it. "It's always been the same."

"That's my point precisely," Obie said. "Why hasn't she changed with the times? It's like we walked onto a set from one of those old TV shows."

"She doesn't have much money," Kyle answered defensively, but then his gaze settled on Mrs. Caine. She hadn't changed her hairstyle or her makeup in all that time. Blue eye shadow still covered her eyelids.

"Lucky for me I had three cups out already," Mrs. Caine said and looked up. "Neighbors were supposed to come over, but they canceled at the last minute."

Kyle gave Obie a look. "See, there's an explanation for everything."

"Okay," Obie said and held up his hand, concentrating. A luminous vapor spread over his fingers. Then he wrote three runic symbols in the air: *Du miht wip*. He made the incantation, and the writing glowed, overpowering the coffee aroma with the scent of burning roses.

Mrs. Caine watched but didn't seem troubled by what she saw.

The letters linked together and shot toward her, but instead of dissolving under her skin, the charm raced through her. She squealed, as if it had tickled.

"You're a magician, Obie." Mrs. Caine seemed childlike in her reaction. "How did you make the letters fly?"

"The spell went right through her," Kyle whispered.

"I know that," Obie whispered back,

looking baffled. "Maybe I gave her a dose that was too strong for her."

"Did it work?" Kyle asked, studying Mrs. Caine.

"I don't know." Obie shrugged. "Ask her a question."

"Are you going to join me or not?" Mrs. Caine offered Kyle a cup of coffee.

Kyle stepped over to the couch and sat down next to Mrs. Caine. Obie joined them on the opposite side from Kyle.

"Mrs. Caine," Kyle began. "Can you tell me about my twin?"

The cup and saucer fell from Mrs. Caine's hands and hit the edge of the table with a loud clatter of breaking china. The steaming coffee spilled onto the carpet.

"Are you all right?" Kyle asked, concerned.

She looked down at her hands, too ashamed to look into his eyes. "I was afraid of this," she said. "I tried to keep him from you, but he's not easy to control. I should have known."

"Kent's real?" Obie asked.

She nodded, and finally looked at Kyle. "I lied to you, but I never did it out of mean-spiritedness. I know it's wrong to keep siblings apart, but I was only trying to protect you."

"From what?" Kyle asked, his heart hammering painfully in his chest.

"Your brother," she answered. "He wants to kill you."

CHAPTER TWELVE

"**W**HY?" KYLE ASKED as a dozen other questions raced through his mind. "And why would you think lying to me about him would keep me safe?"

"I was afraid that if you knew you really did have a twin, you'd want to see him, and he's evil," Mrs. Caine said. "He could have manipulated you into believing he was your friend, all the while waiting for the opportunity to . . ." She grabbed Kyle's hand, and her unexpected touch made him flinch. "I have such nightmares about what he would do to you if he had the chance."

Mrs. Caine sank back on the couch, her

face colorless and stricken, as if she were reliving unpleasant memories. "He's too strong for me to control now, but I can tell you the truth. When you were taken from me, Kent came to live with me, only then I didn't know that you had a twin, I thought he was you."

The clatter of silverware on china made Kyle glance up. Obie held the sugar bowl and was hungrily spooning sugar into his mouth. Kyle didn't bother to stop him; Mrs. Caine was too lost in thought to notice his odd behavior.

"I thought you had returned to me," Mrs. Caine continued, still gazing off into the distance. "He pretended to be you, and why should I have doubted him? The two of you looked exactly the same. He said he'd run away from the new foster home down in Long Beach because he was unhappy there."

Kyle remembered the foster home in Belmont Shores. He tried to recall if he had seen Kent there.

"I believed Kent was you," Mrs. Caine said. "Of course, we believe what we want to be true, and I wanted you back here, safe, with me. Kent fooled me, but not for long. He wasn't like you at all. He was belligerent and unkind, setting fires and throwing stones at the neighborhood cats and dogs." She paused and looked at Kyle. "You were always the perfect child, so good."

"Perfect?" Obie chuckled, interrupting his sugar feed. Kyle shot him a censoring look.

"Kent's still living with you, isn't he?" Kyle asked.

She nodded. "He scares me. I've tried to get away from him so many times, but I always end up back here. It's my home, I know, but *he* won't leave." Mrs. Caine stood and started toward the back of the house. "I want to show you something."

"Could Kent have that kind of power over her?" Kyle whispered to Obie.

"You mean to cast a spell that would keep Mrs. Caine bound to him?" Obie asked as they followed Mrs. Caine down a dim hallway. "Sure. Why not? It's done all the time." Obie shrugged; to him magic was commonplace.

The fragrance of Kent's aftershave became stronger as they approached the bedroom, but underneath that smell Kyle caught a whiff of bitter orange, and the scent brought back memories of the nightmares of his youth. He started to ask about the citrus scent, but Mrs. Caine spoke first. "Look at what Kent has done."

Kyle and Obie stepped into the room and stood transfixed before a mural painted in muddy tones—except for the red that colored the blood and the flaming halo around a beautiful woman warrior. Chaotic scenes of a war between beasts and humans covered all four walls. The surging motion and artistic power awed Kyle, but the carnage repelled him. Something about the picture seemed familiar. He wondered vaguely if Kent had copied it from another painting.

"That's worse than anything I saw in Nefandus," Obie whispered. His master had been a scholar, and Obie was the only one of the four who had seen the treasured artifacts in the museums there. "The landscape and buildings look like Agarttha."

"Where's that?" Kyle asked.

"It's a mythical place," Obie explained.

"It's supposedly the spiritual center of the universe. Lots of books have been written about it in Nefandus. The master had one with detailed drawings."

"Wherever it is, it's scary to think that this is what Kent sees in his imagination," Kyle said, studying the large central figures, and then he added, in a low tone so Mrs. Caine couldn't hear him, "Could he know something about the plans of Nefandus to invade the earth realm?"

Obie nodded. "It's possible. It definitely looks like a war between two worlds."

The thick black lines outlining the center beast drew Kyle's eyes upward to an odd arrangement of stars. "Do you think the alignment means something?"

"Absolutely," Obie said and traced his fingers from one star to the next. "But I don't recognize the constellation, if that's what it is."

"We need Ashley," Kyle said. "I never thought I'd ever say that, but she understands the influence of the stars and planets. She'll know what this means."

"Maybe that has been her connection to

Kent all along," Obie added, and then something else caught his attention, and he knelt, brushing the baseboard with his hand. "He's written a runic inscription."

"I tried to erase it," Mrs. Caine said from behind them, her voice higher and more distraught. "He told me it was a curse to weaken Kyle's spirit."

Kyle stared at the ancient lettering. The arcane words vibrated, and he knew intuitively that his gaze had awakened them. The symbols started to move, squirming around one another. He looked at Obie. "What is it?"

"She's right. It's a hex, but now that we know, we can do something about it." Obie stood and carved an inscription in the air. The fragrance of burning roses filled the room as the words grew large with golden energy. The letters rustled softly, trying to move. But even when Obie flung his hand out, the words remained fixed where Obie had written them.

"What's wrong?" Kyle asked.

"Something's holding my spell." Obie lifted his hand again, but before he could do anything, a black vapor encircled his incantation. The letters crackled and sputtered, then withered, dying, and dissolved into ash. The scent of citrus overpowered the floral fragrance and made Kyle's eyes sting.

Obie looked worried. "I don't have the power to counteract his force. Something has given him strong magic, but where'd he get it?"

Mrs. Caine stepped closer to Kyle. "Kent blames you for abandoning him. He goes on and on, telling me all the promises you made and broke. I'm so worried for you. I know he has something terrible planned."

Kyle turned back and studied the painting. His mouth had gone dry, and he felt a flood of new anxiety.

"It's okay," Obie said. "Now that we know you've been hexed, we can find a way to counteract it."

But Kyle felt the curse settle over him. He believed that a telepathic network connected everyone on some deep level. Mostly people were unaware of this connection, and they didn't understand how their thoughts and words could harm or help another. When he glanced up at the mural again, he saw his own end. This was his future.

"We better find Samuel and Berto and tell them what we know," Obie said, starting out of the room.

Kyle followed him, but paused and put his arm around Mrs. Caine. "Do you want to come with us?" Kyle asked. He was concerned for her safety.

"No," she answered, drawing away from him. "This is my home."

"Are you going to be all right alone?" Obie asked.

"I can't go with you," she said firmly. "It's no use. I've tried to leave a thousand times, but I always end up back here. I'm certain Kent's cast a spell over me, too. It feels as if he's hexed me, anyway."

At the door, Obie turned abruptly. "Mrs. Caine, why did they take Kyle away from you? Your home seems like such a perfect place for a kid to live."

She faltered, uncertain. "The social worker claimed I didn't have a license," she said at last. "Can you imagine that? I needed some paper or other to care for Kyle. I told her that love should have been authorization enough, but she threatened to call the police if I didn't turn Kyle over to her and let him go back to his own home. I thought his foster mother didn't seem very fit."

"I remember her," Kyle said, looking through the bank of trees at the house down the street. "But I didn't stay with her very long after that. The social worker placed me in a home down in Long Beach."

Obie stood on the porch, not budging. "But if Kyle wasn't placed here, then how did he end up with you?"

Mrs. Caine looked at Kyle with adoration. "He just wandered down to my house one day like a poor little stray. Of course I took him in, the dear child. You should have seen him."

"I don't remember that." Kyle started to kiss Mrs. Caine good-bye, but then he remembered his encounter with the police. He hurriedly explained to Mrs. Caine everything that had happened.

When he had finished, she spoke. "Don't worry. I'll go down the street to the pay phone and call the police. Maybe they'll even come by so I can talk to them. But I'll let them know one way or another that they want your brother, not you."

"Thanks," Kyle said. Then he hugged Mrs. Caine good-bye and headed toward the street, with Obie beside him.

"Instead of answers, I have more questions than I had before," Obie said as he opened the car door.

Kyle stared back at the house. "I know."

"I think a powerful magic is working here," Obie said. "One I can't identify."

"I feel the same way," Kyle offered. He wondered what Kent was. He couldn't rid himself of the odd sense of foreboding that had begun when he first looked at the mural; he felt something immeasurably evil lurking in the future, impatiently waiting for him.

CHAPTER THIRTEEN

WHEN OBIE AND Kyle arrived back in Chinatown, a black Mercedes was parked illegally in front of their apartment building, the front wheels planted on the curb as though the driver had thought about ramming the building but had stopped inches from the door. Dora paced near the car, her heels tapping an angry staccato rhythm on the concrete. Her hair was mussed, strands of bleached blond sticking up on end from having raked her fingers over her scalp.

"There you are," she shouted when Kyle climbed out of his Impala. "Get in my car. We still have time for you to make Wardrobe and be on the set for the first call."

"Dora, there's a lot I need to talk to you about," Kyle said. "I'm not sure I'm really the one the director wants."

"Stage fright? Is that what this is about?" She lifted her sunglasses, and her gaze zeroed in on Kyle. "Don't go weird on me now. You owe me. I vouched for you and lied about your age, and I'm not going to let you ruin my reputation in this town. Do you know how hard it is to become a successful casting director?"

"Go with her." Obie nudged Kyle and opened the car door for him. "I'll tell the others what happened."

"I didn't really get the part," Kyle muttered. "Kent did. Besides, I don't know the lines, and what if the police show up?"

"Mrs. Caine promised she'd take care of that," Obie said. "And you've studied the lines enough. I know you have them memorized."

"Get in, Kyle," Dora ordered as she slid behind the steering wheel. She turned the key in the ignition and gunned the engine.

Kyle climbed in as Dora spun the steering wheel. The car made a tight U-turn and sped away with a screech of tires.

Minutes later, Kyle stood in Wardrobe, staring at his reflection in a dusty full-length mirror while the costume designer added Gucci cuff links to his white shirt.

The production assistant opened the trailer door and peered inside, her curly hair flying. "Didn't you go to Makeup yet?" She didn't wait for an answer. The door flapped closed and she returned with the makeup artist, a bald, heavyset man. He powdered Kyle's face with bronzer and brushed his hair as they walked to the set.

Two hours later, the scene still wasn't complete.

"Cut," the director yelled for the seventh time in a row.

The script supervisor tapped her pencil impatiently on the armrest of her chair. The extras and actors were sweating, and Kyle felt his own makeup seeping into his shirt collar. He swallowed hard, self-consciously aware that he was the reason everyone was still standing in the sweltering sunshine.

The director stepped onto the set, put a fatherly hand on Kyle's shoulder, and guided him away to a shaded area. "I picked you because your audition was by far the best."

"I guess I'm just not the same person today," Kyle said glumly, wishing he had had the right to say thank you; but it had been Kent's performance that the director had seen.

"Sometimes, when the cameras are rolling, there's too much pressure to perform," the director said softly. "Do you want to call it quits?"

Kyle shook his head. Even though Kent had won the part, this was his opportunity. He didn't know why he felt so nervous. But then, suddenly he did: he was afraid he would fail. "Give me one last chance," Kyle said determinedly.

"Collect yourself," the director said. "Then come back."

When Kyle stepped in front of the camera again, his heartbeat was thundering in his ears, but this time he breezed through his lines, and at the end the director shouted, "Cut and print!"

Kyle tore off his tie and hurried back to Wardrobe. He turned in his clothes, dressed in his own, then headed to the craft service table for a snack, his stomach rumbling hungrily.

He was surprised to see Berto leaning against the white catering truck waiting for him.

"How'd you get in?" Kyle asked, taking a cookie from the spread.

"The security guard recognized me." Berto smiled broadly. "I'm practically part of L.A. culture since I've been working at Quake. He told me he'd let me on the set if I'd get his daughter and her friends into the club on Tuesday night when their favorite singer goes there."

"Did Obie—"

"Obie and Samuel told me everything," Berto interrupted. "And I agree with Samuel. I think you really do have a brother, but I don't understand how you let others convince you that you don't."

"It's complicated," Kyle began slowly.

"Doc Witherspoon told me that my loneliness had created Kent. He said that sometimes when people are really sad they hallucinate and see things that aren't there. I didn't believe him at first, but when you're a kid and an adult tells you something over and over again, you start to believe what you're told."

"Why were you so sad?" Berto asked, his dark eyes probing.

"I was an outcast." Kyle took a slice of bread and spooned pickle relish on top. "I didn't have any friends except for the ones I imagined in my head."

"But everyone likes you now," Berto said, even though that wasn't necessarily true. "What was going on then?"

Kyle grabbed the mustard. "I was always in trouble for something."

"So, even back then Kent was doing things and pretending to be you."

"It's a possibility," Kyle agreed.

Berto tossed an olive into his mouth. "I wonder why he's waited until now to come back into your life."

"I don't know." Kyle shook his head. "But I don't think he's real. I know he exists, but not the way you and I do. He wasn't breathing."

"Are you sure?" Berto asked. "You would have been so stunned to see your twin that you probably weren't breathing right, either."

Kyle added a slice of onion to his sandwich, then paused and looked at Berto. "I know how we can find out if my impression is real. He's probably over at Ashley's, hanging out with her."

Berto's eyes flashed with emotion.

"He's the one you saw with her, not me," Kyle went on. "We could spy on them and see if he's breathing or not."

"I'll go," Berto said. "Watch my body."

"Wait," Kyle said as a transparent replica started to leave through Berto's forehead. Berto winced as his spirit slipped back into his body.

"I'll go with you," Kyle said. "We'll turn to shadow and—"

"It'll take too long to float over to Santa Monica," Berto argued. "Besides, Ashley watches shadows. She's hyperalert because she knows she's made powerful people on the other side angry. She'd see us as soon as we arrived. Sending my spirit is the only way. I'll be a speck of consciousness. She'll never see me; neither will Kent."

Kyle glanced at the crew lined up at the side of the catering truck, waiting for hot meals. "All right," he agreed, but when he glanced back, Berto's spirit had already left. A barely visible thread of silvery light wavered in the air, anchoring Berto's soul to his body. Kyle edged in front of Berto, trying to hide him so no one passing would notice his blank face and stiff body.

He started to take a bite of sandwich when he felt someone behind him and turned. "Emily! What are you doing here?"

"My dad's the line producer." She stepped to the other side of the table. Her sunny smile vanished. She frowned and looked at Berto. "What's wrong with him?"

"He's meditating," Kyle answered, reaching for the first answer that came into his mind.

"I meditate, but I've never seen anyone

look so . . . well, dead." She started to grab the delicate thread. "What's this?"

Kyle dropped his sandwich and grabbed her hand before she could touch the cord. Berto had told Kyle that it was the only thing connecting his soul to his body, and that if anyone ever severed it, he wouldn't be able to find his way back.

"Aren't you afraid of spiders?" Kyle asked, stepping over to her side of the table.

"That doesn't look like a spiderweb." She glanced down at the mustard and pickle relish Kyle had accidentally smeared on her fingers.

"Sorry." Kyle grabbed a napkin and handed it to her. "Haven't you ever seen a ballooning spider?" He stepped in front of her, blocking her view of Berto, and hurried on, changing the subject. "I was hoping to see you. I wanted to explain about Ashley and apologize."

She licked at the mustard on her fingers and cocked her head in a flirty way. "How many times do you think you have to say you're sorry?"

"So you accepted my apology?" he asked,

feeling foolish. Kent must have spoken to her already, but when had he had a chance to talk to her? And why was he so concerned about keeping Emily happy? Instead of feeling grateful, Kyle worried, wondering what Kent's real motive was.

"I thought about it, and you're right. Everyone knows what Ashley does. She thrives on making other people jealous."

"And when I kissed Ashley there on the street," Kyle went on, wondering how Kent had explained their embrace. "You understand about that, too?"

Emily shrugged. "You're an actor. You were going over your lines with Ashley, and she was making a big production of it because she knew you liked me and she was trying to make me jealous to split us up. That's so like her."

"I'm glad you understand." Kyle admired Kent's ability to lie. He was a master. But it wasn't a trait Kyle wanted to emulate.

"My dad said I could use his car," Emily said, after a short pause. "Let's go over to Little Tokyo and get some mochi ice cream."

"I'd love to," Kyle said. "But I can't."

The corner of her mouth twitched. "Why not? I know you finished your scene."

"I want to go with you," Kyle answered. "I really do, but . . ." What could he say? She'd never have believed him if he had told her the truth, and there was no way he was going to leave Berto's vacated body unattended.

She scowled.

"Look," he said, stalling as he raced through his thoughts trying to find an excuse. "This is really embarrassing, but I was hoping I'd get a chance to talk to the star. I've always admired him and—"

"You're lying," she said emphatically. "Everyone knows he's not on the set today. I hate a liar more than anything. I'd rather hear the truth even if it hurts my feelings."

"I can't tell you the truth," he said finally. "And *that's* the truth."

"Because you don't trust me?" she asked. "Or because the truth involves another girl? You're meeting someone, aren't you? I bet it's Ashley. I'm such a fool."

"I'm not meeting anyone," he said. "Can't we go out later?"

"I gave you a second chance and then a third, because sometimes I really like you, but right now I think you're pathetic." She stormed off.

He started after her, but then a soft whistle filled the air and he turned back. The silver thread quivered, catching the sunlight. Berto's translucent double appeared and entered his body.

"You're right," Berto said, blinking to readjust his vision for the correct plane. "Kent isn't alive. He's like the walking dead. He doesn't breathe, and if he has a heart, it isn't beating."

"How did you find out?" Kyle said, gratified someone believed him, but also wanting to hear the details.

"I pressed my ear against his chest," Berto answered and wheezed, giving Kyle the impression that his spirit still wanted to soar and was having a hard time settling.

"He didn't sense you?" Kyle asked.

Berto shook his head. "He was too busy studying astrological charts with Ashley."

"The mural," Kyle said, wondering what they had been looking for in the star maps.

Berto nodded. "Obie told me about the alignment of stars that Kent had painted on the wall," Berto said. "But that's not what bothers me. Ashley was leaning close to Kent. She should have noticed that he wasn't really breathing. So why didn't she?"

"Maybe she is aware, but she isn't worried, because she's using him to get the diamond," Kyle offered. "More than anything, she wants to go back to her own time, and the diamond would give her the power she needs." He had never told Berto the reason she so desperately wanted to travel back to ancient Mesopotamia; he didn't tell him now about the Tablet of Destinies that she had stolen and hidden.

"I'm afraid she's in danger," Berto said. "We need to stop Kent. Ashley may think she's using him, but I don't trust him. I have a feeling he's using her."

"I know," Kyle said. "But we have to find out what he is before we can figure out how to stop him."

CHAPTER FOURTEEN

THE NEXT MORNING, Kyle, Obie, Berto, and Samuel waited on the steps of the Bodhi Tree bookstore. The heat from the morning sun was already radiating off the blue stucco walls with the promise of more sweltering heat to come in spite of the red Christmas bells and the tinsel hanging from the lampposts. When the door finally opened, Obie was the first inside. Kyle followed, breathing the incense-scented air. The old wooden floorboards squeaked under their footsteps.

"What are we looking for, exactly?" Samuel whispered from near the magazine rack. He looked eager to get back outside.

"I'm not sure," Kyle said, already feeling frustrated by the task ahead of them.

"How can we find something when we don't know what it is we're searching for?" Berto asked, staring at the brightly painted statues of Hindu gods in a display case.

"It might take all day," Kyle answered. "But if we don't find it here, I don't know where we'll find it."

"But find what?" Samuel asked, picking up a book and setting it back as if he wished he were any place but there.

"I'm hoping there's a book that will explain what Kent is," Kyle tried again. "And more specifically, something that will tell us how to get rid of him."

"In a book?" Berto looked doubtful. "Why aren't we confronting Kent? There are four of us and only one of him."

"Because he could use the black diamond against us," Obie said, looking around. "It's too bad they don't have the Akashic Records in the public library."

The others stopped and stared at him.

"What's that?" Samuel asked.

"It's a collection of books that contain all the knowledge of humankind from the beginning to the end of time. My master had a few volumes, and he was always trying to get more."

"We have got to go back into Nefandus and see what the books say about us," Kyle said. "At least then maybe we'd know what we're supposed to do."

"Or how we're supposed to die," Samuel added glumly. "I don't want to know what's going to happen."

"Next trip, you and Obie can read," Berto said moodily. "Samuel and I'll fight off the Regulators." He started away from them, staring up at the framed pictures of saints mounted high on the walls above the bookcases.

"Meet you back here in an hour," Kyle said, and he walked away. He wandered to the back, drawn for no reason that he understood to a small alcove. He stepped inside, edging around the wooden stool that was used to reach the books on the top shelves, and began reading the titles. He had only been there a few minutes when he felt another customer crowd in behind him. He started to move out of the way when a warm hand touched his back.

"Why don't you try traditional Tibetan doctrines?" a voice said. "I think you'll find what you're looking for there."

Kyle spun around.

The monk who had helped him escape from Nefandus stood behind him, his face hidden under the hood of his cloak.

"How did you know I'd be here?" Kyle asked, excited. But as he started to embrace him, he stopped and pulled back. Something was definitely wrong. The monk was too short and too thin. Kyle clearly remembered that the monk had been at least as tall as he was, and that the material of his cloak had been of rough, homespun fabric. The robe he was wearing now was sewn from gray polyester and looked flimsy, like a costume someone would wear for Halloween.

"Who are you?" Kyle asked, fear rising with his suspicions.

The monk turned his head, seeming to be afraid that Kyle might see his face. "Does it matter?" the monk asked, obviously trying to lower his voice. "I have the answer to your questions."

"Do you know what Kent is?" Kyle whispered.

The monk nodded and moved around Kyle, intent on finding a book. At last he pulled one from the shelf, but as he thumbed through the pages, his hands were exposed. The delicate fingers definitely belonged to a woman.

Kyle stepped forward and pushed back the cowl.

A woman gasped and looked up at him. She had a pleasant look, even though her skin was deadly pale. Her long golden hair curled over her shoulders.

"You're not the one who helped me escape," Kyle said.

"Obviously, I'm not," she said, pulling the hood back over her head. "But everyone in

Nefandus has heard of the monk, so I used him for my disguise. I didn't want you to see me. I wanted to come and go anonymously."

"Why?" Kyle asked.

"Because," she said, still not looking at him, "I'm your mother, and it's dangerous for you to know me."

CHAPTER FIFTEEN

KYLE STAGGERED BACK and collapsed on the stool, his legs suddenly too weak to hold him. He stared up at the woman who claimed to be his mother and recognized himself in the color of her hair, the fullness of her mouth, and the dimples in her sad smile. He had imagined meeting his mother one day and had spent many sleepless hours before dawn practicing what he would say to her, but now words failed him. He was too afraid if he did open his mouth that a sob would be the only sound to come out. He clenched his jaw to stop his chin from quivering.

She must have sensed his mixed emotions, but she didn't put her arms around him and soothe him as he would have thought a mother should.

"Why are you here now, after all these years?" Kyle said at last, surprised by the anger in his voice.

"I've come to help you," she said, but she didn't move to comfort him.

"Have you known where I was since you abandoned me?"

"I didn't abandon you," she answered sharply, silencing him. Their eyes locked, and he wondered whether what she was saying could be true. Had something else separated them?

"The night you were born I escaped from Nefandus and took you with me," she began. "Regulators chased me into the earth realm. I was terrified they were going to catch us. It was you they wanted, not me. They knew I'd go back. I hid you in a Dumpster and grabbed an alley cat and turned us both to shadow, hoping its heartbeat would deceive them into believing I still carried you in my arms."

Kyle's anger slowly turned to admiration for the woman standing before him. "And then?"

"I succeeded in leading them away from you, but by the time I was able to return, someone had already found you and taken you to the hospital. Part of me was relieved. I sensed you were safe, your true identity unknown, but my heart was also broken because I had lost you."

"Were you a *serva*?" Kyle asked.

"No, but I suppose I might as well have been one." She seemed unsure and hesitated. "I met your father in Los Angeles and fell in love with him. I thought he was an ordinary man. He worked as a lineman for the telephone company and seemed real enough."

"Real?" Kyle stood, ignoring his light-headedness, and stepped closer to his mother. "He's not human?"

The look in her eyes was all the answer he needed. He grabbed the shelf to steady himself, ignoring the sliver that slipped painfully into his thumb.

"By the time I found out what he was, I

was already pregnant with you," she explained.

"What is he?" Kyle whispered, clutching his throat; the air seemed to have thickened, clogging his lungs.

She looked down at her hands and absently rubbed at a tattoo on her ring finger. "Your father had only one request," she said. "From our wedding night on—"

"You married him?" Kyle asked, wondering if the snake tattooed around her finger had been part of the ceremony.

"I didn't know what he was then," she said forcefully. "After we were married, he asked that I never look at him while he was sleeping. His request seemed odd, but I was so in love with him that I did as he said, until one night when we had a small earthquake. The tremor woke me, and when I turned on the lights to see if there was any damage, your father wasn't in bed. I thought he must have gotten up to get a glass of water, so I got up and started for the kitchen but when I reached the door, he called my name from behind me."

She paused, as if even now she could feel

the terror she had felt then. "He was on the bed, sprawled on top of the covers. I didn't say anything, but the next night I stayed awake, waiting until he was asleep; then I took my flashlight and shone the beam on him. He wasn't there—at least, I couldn't see him—but when I reached out, my fingers ran over his arm, his hair." She shuddered. "My touch awakened him and he suddenly materialized. At first I thought he was a ghost."

"What is he?" Kyle asked impatiently when she paused.

"One of the first demons created from the cosmic dust," she whispered. "The night I discovered what he was he took me to live in Nefandus."

Kyle winced. "You're still married to him, aren't you?" He didn't need an answer; he knew with certainty that she was.

"I love him," she whispered and looked down, seeming ashamed. "I can't help it."

"And me?" Kyle asked.

She looked up. "Of course I love you, too. That's why I'm here now, in spite of the risk.

You need my help, and so do others. Things in Nefandus are desperate for those who want peace. There has been a terrible shift in power since the Daughters of the Moon were captured."

Kyle felt a new wave of anxiety wash over him. Catty was a Daughter of the Moon, a goddess. She had worried that if people learned her secret, the government would take her to some remote military base and study her. She had imagined herself undergoing tests and possibly dissection, so scientists could understand her power. But even more than that, she had feared being captured by the Atrox, the ancient evil that ruled Nefandus, and now her worst nightmare had come true.

"Many people in Nefandus love Catty and pray she'll make the right decision," his mother continued. "They see her as their only hope."

"When you say, 'the right decision,' do you mean, for good or for evil?" Kyle asked.

"Catty has unimaginable power that was meant for good," his mother answered. "But rumors are circulating that her father has convinced her to fight with him rather than on the side of light."

"Never," Kyle said sharply. "I know Catty better than that. She would never help her father invade the earth realm. Even if she did somehow choose to side with him, the other Daughters would stop her before she could do anything."

"How can they?" his mother asked. "Catty is living with her father, separated from the other two Daughters."

"Only two?" Kyle asked, surprised.

"Vanessa and Serena are in prison," his mother answered. "No one knows where. People speculate and gossip about their location, but most think they've been enslaved and live with the Atrox."

Kyle could feel his apprehension growing. The Daughters and their powers were the only force that had kept the Atrox from invading the earth realm, and he wondered what would happen to the world without their protection. "What about Tianna and Jimena?"

"Tianna sacrificed herself to weaken the

Atrox so it could no longer take human form," his mother said. "And Jimena is still discovering her true identity as the reincarnation of Pandia. Neither of them can help."

"But Jimena should be doing something," Kyle said. His thoughts kept turning back to Catty; he imagined her with her father, who was a member of the Inner Circle.

"Jimena knows that if she does anything to free Catty, either Vanessa or Serena will be sacrificed in retaliation. Everything is at a stalemate right now, and the members of the Inner Circle feel that the only way to shift the balance is to convince Catty to use her powers against you."

"Me?" Kyle asked. "What threat could I possibly pose?"

"Your destiny has been intertwined with Catty's since the three sister Fates sat in the great void at the beginning of time and wove the future, but no one knows if the two of you will end up as enemies or allies."

A terrible cold swept through Kyle and settled in the pit of his stomach. He still cared for Catty. He couldn't imagine what he would do if she turned against him and tried to battle him, but why would she? She had enormously strong powers, while he had only those given to *servi*. Then he remembered what his mother had said about his father, and he glanced down at his hands, wondering if he could really be part demon. If he were, what did that imply?

"You must have misunderstood," he said firmly and looked at his mother, wondering if she had a reason to lie to him. "Catty broke up with me because she was afraid it was too dangerous for me to be seen with her. She was concerned for my safety."

His mother shook her head. "Catty discovered your true identity before you knew."

"She knew I was part demon?" he asked, feeling his heart beat painfully inside his chest. Why hadn't Catty told him?

"She discovered you were one of the Four of Legend." His mother held up her hand to silence him, and tilted her head as if listening for something. "My time with you is running out. For now, you must keep what I've told you secret."

"Why?"

"Don't you understand the danger yet?" she asked impatiently. "If those in power know who have this knowledge, they'll assume you'll try to rescue Catty."

"But I will."

"You can't. Catty must make her own decision and if you try to rescue her you'll only make matters worse," his mother said emphatically, but even as she spoke Kyle sensed the lie underneath her words. Why was she trying to keep him from going into Nefandus to rescue Catty?

"If Catty needs me—"

"Don't you understand anything?" She looked at him as if she were disappointed in his foolishness. She opened the book she had been holding and ran her finger down the page. "Read this so you'll know what Kent is."

Kyle took the book and read out loud: *"According to Tibetan belief, a* tulpa *can be created from vivid imagination, concentration, and visualization. The creature first appears as a ghost but continues to grow until it becomes indistinguishable from any other substance in physical reality. If the* tulpa *becomes strong enough, it can slip away from its creator's conscious control and gain the power to come and go without its creator willing it.*" Kyle looked up at his mother. "Kent is a *tulpa*?"

"He was an illusion, your imaginary friend," his mother stated. "But the more you envisioned him, the stronger he grew. Now he has become self-aware, and he's trying to give himself the breath of life. You must destroy him before his heart beats."

"No wonder he hates me," Kyle said, closing the book. "He's afraid I'll call him back into nonexistence. But how do I destroy something that doesn't really exist?"

A pink aura began encircling his mother, and she glanced behind her, seeming terrified someone might see. "I'm being forced to leave," she whispered.

"Who's calling you back?" Kyle asked.

"A friend who helped me find you. Someone must have noticed that I was gone," she answered, pulling the hood back over her face. "You are in terrible danger both from your power and from those that want to destroy your power."

"I have a power?" he asked.

"Don't be foolish," she answered. "Only one thing will save you. You must remember that hatred cannot be conquered by hatred, but by love alone is destroyed. Say those words for me."

Kyle repeated the words, wondering how that could save him. When he had finished, she nodded, as if satisfied that he understood, then started to dissolve into the pink aura. He grabbed her sleeve, forcing her to stay longer.

"Tell me my real name," he said. "The nurses in the hospital called me Kyle, but what did you name me?"

"There is danger in knowing your real name," she whispered, her eyes widening with fear. "Don't try to find out what it is."

"What harm could come from knowing my name?" he asked.

Sudden footsteps made the floorboards creak, and she brushed his hand away. "You'll find out your true name soon enough. Promise me that you won't be foolhardy and put my happiness at risk."

"Your happiness?" he asked.

"You," she answered simply. "I couldn't tolerate more sorrow."

"I wish you had come to me sooner," he said plaintively. "Anything, even growing up in Nefandus, would have been better than the life I endured."

But the look in her eyes told him that in fact his life would have been immeasurably worse if he had stayed with her. Before he could question her more, she faded into the nimbus surrounding her.

Berto stepped into the alcove. "What did you find?" he asked, looking at the book in Kyle's hand.

"I know what Kent is," Kyle said and showed Berto the description of a *tulpa*.

Obie and Samuel crowded into the cramped space with them. Kyle didn't tell them about his mother's visit. Her warning kept replaying in his mind. He wasn't sure if she had told him the truth, but he needed time to absorb everything she had said before he told his friends about her or about his father. He glanced down at his hands again, studying the skin and nails, searching for evidence of his heritage. He felt possessed by something alien and ugly.

"Kent is a *tulpa*," Berto said, glancing up from the open book and interrupting Kyle's thoughts. "An entity created by intense concentration and visualization. Some people speculate that the Loch Ness monster and bigfoot are actually *tulpas*."

"That makes perfect sense," Samuel said with authority. "Our thoughts create electromagnetic and chemical changes inside our brains, so it stands to reason that if millions of people believe in something their thoughts could generate enough energy to bring it into existence."

Obie and Berto stared at him. "How do you know that?" Obie asked.

Samuel shrugged. "Kyle signed me up for all these science classes when he made me start high school."

Obie took the book and started skimming

through the pages. "According to this, the only way to destroy Kent is for Kyle to absorb him."

"Does that mean *unthink* him?" Kyle said, feeling overwhelmed by all the facts he had just learned. "It's hard to believe I imagined him."

"But you said yourself he wasn't breathing," Samuel said. "Look at my power animals. They seem real, yet we know they can't exist as animals do in nature, anyway. Where do they go when they're not with me? Maybe Kent came from the same place."

"I'm not aware of having any special power," Kyle said. "Why would I have been able to create something then and not now?"

"When you were a kid you probably used your power, and back then it was normal for you," Obie explained. "But then adults like Doc Witherspoon started telling you that it was impossible for you to do what you were doing, and that made you doubt yourself, and you stopped believing in your abilities."

Kyle paused, remembering the conversations he'd had with social workers and therapists.

"Now you have to find the source of that

power again so you can uncreate Kent," Berto said.

"That sounds easy enough," Kyle agreed. "But I don't know if I can, and Kent doesn't seem like the type of supernatural creature who will easily give up his existence."

"We might have a bigger problem," Obie cautioned, looking up from the book again. "It says here that once the *tulpa* becomes self-aware, it will try to destroy its creator."

"Do you think that's why Kent has come back into my life now?" Kyle asked, and the grim expressions on his friends' faces told him that it was.

CHAPTER SIXTEEN

CHRISTMAS CAROLS and laughter came from the backyard of the tree-sheltered house behind Kyle. He crouched beside the SUV parked in the drive and breathed deeply, relishing the smoky smells of barbecued meat. He spit his gum into the gutter, suddenly dissatisfied with its stale flavor, and stared across the street at Catty's house, the evening air cool against his face.

Three days had passed since the visit with his mother, and a dreamlike fog had shrouded his memory. He could barely recall his mother's face, but what she had said about Catty remained clear. Had she told him the truth? He had tried to contact Catty, leaving messages on her answering machine and sending e-mails, but so far he had received no response.

That morning he had driven over to her house, determined to speak to either Catty or her mother, Kendra, but each time he had started up the walk, the air surrounding the porch had quivered, as if the membrane dividing Nefandus from the earth realm had suddenly become permeable there.

Finally he had left, deciding to wait until nightfall to return, hoping the curious heat waves had been no more than a trick of sunlight and too much imagination on his part. But already he sensed that something was wrong. He angled across the street like a thief, watching Catty's house for movement inside.

Silver garlands looped across the porch, swinging lazily, even though the night was still, without a breeze. He hesitated, wondering what made the holiday decorations sway. When the motion stopped, he crossed the porch, his footsteps pounding hollowly, and glanced up at the eaves. The wind chimes had been taken down, replaced by blinking Christmas lights.

A reindeer with a red nose grinned at him from a wreath hanging on the door. The decoration didn't seem like something Kendra would have put up. He started to ring the doorbell but pulled back, sensing that someone was watching him. The sound of footsteps running stealthily made him whirl around. He expected to see a silhouette duck behind the oleander bushes, but he saw no one. He pressed back, feeling exposed, and studied the shadows, cursing silently; he was certain Kent had followed him and was hiding nearby.

The door opened behind him. Warm air from inside rushed around him and when he turned, he stood face to face with a bearded man he had never seen before.

"Is Catty home?" Kyle asked, doubting that this scruffy man could be a friend of Kendra's.

The man looked puzzled. He took off his glasses and cleaned the spotted lenses with the tail of his shirt. "Catty doesn't live here now," he said and put the wire-rimmed frames back on his face. He started to close the door.

Kyle placed his palm flat against the door and stopped the man from closing it. "Can I speak to Kendra, then?" he asked. "It's important."

The man poked his head outside, straining to look up and down the street. Kyle sensed the man's nervousness and followed the man's gaze, trying to see what was making him so edgy.

"I've tried calling—" Kyle started.

"You're Kyle." A flicker of recognition crossed the man's face. "I kept Kendra's phone number in case Catty tried to call home, but Kendra doesn't live here anymore, either."

"Do you know what happened to them?" Kyle asked, desperate to learn more.

The man leaned closer until Kyle could smell the coffee on his breath. "You remember that bad thunderstorm we had?" the man whispered.

Kyle nodded and wondered why the man was whispering. Did he think someone was listening?

"Catty ran away that night, and afterward the house made Kendra uneasy. She decided to move to San Diego. I offered to buy her house before she got a realtor involved. She warned me not to live here, so I can't blame her—"

"Warned you?" Kyle broke in.

The man nodded. "Kendra believed in the mysteries of life—"

"In the occult, you mean," Kyle interrupted again.

The man nodded. "I didn't think much about her warnings. Now I know I should have listened to her. Hindsight, you know."

"Can you give me her number in San Diego?" Kyle asked.

The man looked skeptical, and his suspicion seemed to shift from the street to Kyle. "You give me your number, and I'll ask her if she wants to call you." His request seemed half apologetic. "You know, in this day and age . . ."

"I understand." Kyle pulled out his wallet. He had the growing sense that this man was worried not about thieves and stalkers, but about otherworldly creatures. What had Kendra told him? He handed over one of the business cards he used for his art and acting.

The man took it and, without saying more, hurried back inside, slamming the door. Kyle waited, hoping the man would change his mind and return with Kendra's number, but when the dead bolt slid into place, Kyle started down the walk. At the curb, the sound of the door opening again made him turn back.

The man rushed after him, his face ashen. He handed over a white envelope. *Kyle* was written across the front, in Catty's handwriting. The flap had been sealed with purple wax and stamped with the crest used only by members of the Inner Circle.

"It was on the coffee table when I went back inside," the man said, breathlessly. "I curse the day I bought this house," he muttered; then he rushed back inside.

Kyle tore open the envelope, his heartbeat quickening, and read: "*Ducunt volentem fata, nolentum trahunt.* You can't change what has been decreed. Stay away. Catty."

Kyle translated the Latin as best he could. *The fates lead the willing and drag the unwilling* was what it seemed to say. He didn't need a precise translation. He had heard the phrase often enough in Nefandus to know Catty was telling him that no matter what he did, he couldn't change their destinies; the outcome was going to be the same. But was her note a warning, or an apology for the fact that they were destined to become enemies?

CHAPTER SEVENTEEN

ON FRIDAY MORNING, an odd smell woke Kyle. He buried his head under his pillow and pressed his nose into the mattress, trying to return to his dream; he had been flying, soaring higher and higher over the ocean, carefree and happy.

A tapping against the headboard made him groan.

"Can't you guys let me sleep?" He snuggled deeper under the covers. The curious odor was stronger now. He wondered if one of his roommates was cooking again. Once, Berto had fried some bats, and when Kyle had gone into the kitchen to investigate the smell, he had found Berto crunching on tiny, brittle bones. Samuel's squirrel and dumplings had been even worse.

The tapping continued, and a shushing noise joined it. What were his roommates doing? He had no windows in his bedroom, and with the door closed the darkness was complete. He imagined them sneaking in and laying a tray of breakfast on his sheets to entice him out of bed, or worse, maybe trying to surprise him with some strange food and laughing when he gagged.

Not this time, he thought and mischievously flung his covers aside. He had expected to hear dishes crashing to the floor. Instead a soft *whoosh* followed, as if someone were fanning the air. He listened more intently now. If his roommates weren't up to their usual pranks, then who was in the room with him?

He moved his leg, and when he did, his toes touched something warm and wet. He drew his foot back and sat up, startled, fighting an impulse to scream. The stench was over-powering now, a vague blend of vomit and sardines. Worse, he sensed someone moving furtively across the edge of his bed.

"Berto?" he called, hoping that Berto had projected his spirit into the room. That would have explained the stealthy motion and muted noise, but not the smell. He leaned over his nightstand and switched on the lamp, fearing he'd turn to find a congregation of Regulators gathered behind him.

Bright light momentarily blinded him.

"What the—" he shot back against the wall, hitting his head with a loud thud, and stifled a gasp.

Four seagulls marched stiffly across the foot of his bed, circling around a glob of gray jelly that was soaking into the spread. Their feathers were ruffled and spiked, as if someone had attacked them with a blow-dryer. Two more gulls sat perched on his dresser, flapping their wings. The bird on the headboard tapped at the wood. Its beak was blunted, and its webbed feet were melting into greenish gelatin that dripped onto his pillow.

His first thought was of Samuel. Had he left power animals to guard Kyle? If so, these were sick and desperately in need of care from a veterinarian.

"Samuel!" Kyle's voice echoed about the room but didn't seem to startle the birds nor bring his roommates running. Annoyed, Kyle glanced at the clock. It was already eight-thirty. Samuel would have left for school. He had zero period algebra, and most likely Berto and Obie would have gone with him.

"Great," Kyle muttered, realizing that they had left him to clean up the mess. But as he started to get out of bed, a segment of his dream flashed into his mind. He had been soaring over the ocean with a flock of seagulls.

He fell back onto his mattress, his heart hammering, and focused his attention on the birds. His mother had told him that he was in terrible danger from both his power and those who wanted to destroy it. Now he looked at the decaying gulls and wondered if he had created them while dreaming? Was this what she had meant?

His muscles tightened reflexively, speculating on what would have happened if he had dreamed about alligators, rattlesnakes, or Regulators. Would he have awakened to find them crowded around him? And, would they, like Kent, have had a will of their own and attacked him? Except for Kent, Kyle had never created anything before, at least not that he could remember. He tried to think of all the possibilities, but he kept coming back to one conclusion. Somehow he himself had made those birds come to life.

He leaned forward and touched the closest one, then stared in disbelief as it began to fall apart. He closed his eyes, and then opened one, anticipating a gory mound of blood, bone, and entrails oozing across his bedspread, but the bird had decomposed into the same grayish-green matter that already dripped and pooled in big gobs all over his room.

With the tip of his finger, he touched the sticky material. The gluey stuff smelled foul and felt worse. It wiggled as if alive, slithering across his skin before evaporating. He assumed it was ectoplasm, the substance that emanated from the body of a medium while the psychic was in a trance.

Somehow in his sleep he had released his power. Could he do it while awake? He tried to make his mind go still, pushing away all thoughts, and concentrated, focusing on the image of a bird.

Minutes ticked away. Sweat beaded across his forehead. Nothing happened. He was ready to give up when a fine tremor prickled through him. The air began to stir, slowly at first, like nothing more than dust motes swirling in a cloud; soon, flapping wings formed, fanning his face. Plumage grew in layers. Long white feathers formed a tail.

"Yes!" Kyle yelled as joy swept through him. He whooped and jumped from the bed, throwing his arms up and dancing in a touchdown-style celebration; he had unlocked his gift. He couldn't wait to show his roommates what he could do. In his excitement, he had lost his concentration. The wings stopped fluttering and fell to the bed, flopping frantically like fish out of water before disintegrating into slime.

Kyle stared numbly. He couldn't comprehend his power yet, or even understand what it was, exactly, but he knew he could somehow create what he visualized, or at least he thought he could, even though the physical manifestation didn't last long. Now he speculated that his power had been given to him to build bridges and ladders when he and his roommates finally entered Nefandus to fulfill the Legend of the Four.

But then his mother's warning came back to him like a slap, and he plopped down on the edge of the bed. He tried to push her words aside, but her advice settled into his mind, and he remembered the battle he had witnessed between two masters in Nefandus who had fought over the right to claim him as their *servus*. They had conjured monsters to do their fighting for them. Was that the danger his mother had tried to tell him about?

If he was supposed to spawn terrifying beasts to fight off the magical creatures summoned by powerful magicians, then all was lost: his sickly gulls were no match for the fear-provoking monsters the masters could invoke.

Without warning, thudding footsteps broke the silence outside his room. Terror seized Kyle. Had he conjured such a beast by just thinking about the ones he had seen in Nefandus?

CHAPTER EIGHTEEN

CAUTIOUSLY, KYLE gripped the cold doorknob and turned it slowly in his hand; then he eased open the door to his bedroom and peered out. His muscles tensed. A mammoth shadow strode toward him, huffing and rasping. Kyle held his breath in anticipation.

A moment later, the huge, plodding bear came into clear focus, snorting and rolling its head from side to side. The bear stopped in front of Kyle and looked up plaintively. It had arrived with the coyote, and now they didn't know how to get rid of it.

"Sorry, old guy," Kyle said, understanding its mood. But when he reached out to pet the beast, it sniffed and growled deep in its throat, warning Kyle away before it continued forward down the hallway. The burly animal was no threat to Kyle, but all of a sudden he wanted nothing more than to be outside in the sunlight and in the company of his friends.

Soon, Kyle was standing in line with other students waiting to go through the metal detectors at the entrance to Turney High. Kids gathered in small groups, balancing books and paper cups filled with steaming coffee, excitedly making plans and sensing freedom; this was the last day before the winter break.

Kyle glanced around, wishing he could see one of his roommates. They usually grabbed coffee and donuts across the street after zero period, and now he wondered if they had ditched school without telling him. Berto had been pressuring them to go to Ridgecrest for some snowboarding.

Emily saw him and waved. Kyle stared at the sun glinting off her curls and ran his hand across the top of his own head, trying to remember if he had even bothered to brush his hair before leaving the loft.

"Hi," he called and wondered why she seemed so flustered. He tried to keep his eyes on her face as she walked over to him, but her pleated skirt was cut short, and he kept stealing glances at her legs. He swallowed hard, feeling more attracted to her than ever. "Do you still want me to pick you up for Maddie's party tomorrow night?" he asked when she stood beside him.

"How many times are you going to ask?" Emily frowned, as if something important were bothering her. "We need to talk about last night."

"Last night?" His heart sank. What had Kent done now? He was suddenly sorry he hadn't called Emily last week, but he had been busy trying to find out what had happened to Catty. Now he realized he had left her unprotected, and if anything bad had happened, he was to blame. "Should I apologize?"

"It's not your fault." Her gaze settled on

him and made him uneasy. "I wanted to explain about the kiss."

"We kissed?" he asked, intrigued, and in the same moment he felt a flicker of envy. Kent seemed to be much better at dating than Kyle could ever hope to be.

"You have a right to be sarcastic." She adjusted the fringed poncho she wore wrapped around her shoulders.

"I wasn't being sarcastic," he answered and pulled her back against the huge wall that formed the foundation of the students' parking structure. "What is it?"

"I want to explain, but . . ." She took a deep breath. "I know you'll think I'm weird."

"I'd never think that," he assured her.

Emily leaned against the wall, her cheeks glowing in the morning sunshine. "You probably don't know the details about my illness earlier this year."

Now she had his full attention. He probably knew more about what had happened to her than she did. She had succumbed to the hunger of a Renegade named Macduff, who had unintentionally stolen her life force. Afterward, Macduff had been inconsolable, because he had loved Emily. Kyle stared into her large eyes. She was easy to like, maybe even love. Could that be a possibility for them?

"Tell me," he whispered.

She looked out at the street. "I was going with this guy I liked a lot. He took me to the cemetery. I know that sounds creepy, but Maddie is my best friend, after all, and she's been dragging me along on vampire hunts for as long as I can remember, so it's not like it was my first nighttime visit to a graveyard. Macduff was in a big rush to get there, so I just thought he wanted to show me something."

Kyle knew that Macduff must have sensed that Regulators were chasing them. He would have taken Emily to the holy ground of a cemetery, where they'd be safe.

Emily's face reddened. "He kissed me. That's the last thing I remember, until the groundskeeper found me the next day, stumbling around the tombstones."

"Do you think Macduff did something to

you?" he asked, wondering if his own victims had remembered him.

"That's what Maddie wanted to know," Emily said. "She kept insisting that Macduff was a vampire, and that he had sucked my blood. But I didn't have any puncture wounds on my throat. The doctors thought I had some form of pernicious anemia, but . . ." She paused, searching for the right word.

"But you didn't feel ill as much as you felt like your soul was missing," he finished for her, remembering the blank expressions on his victims' faces, their lifeless eyes. An acute sense of guilt settled over him. He tried to forgive himself for what he had done in the past, but he doubted that he would ever be able to forget.

"That's why I pulled away last night," she went on. "It had nothing to do with you. I know it sounds bizarre, but it feels like my illness was somehow connected to that kiss."

"It's okay," Kyle said, feeling happy that Emily hadn't let Kent kiss her. "I understand."

"I'd like . . ." Emily looked away, apparently too embarrassed to complete the sentence.

"What?" he coaxed.

"I'd like to try now," she whispered. Her eyes focused on him in anticipation.

"Here?" His free hand slid down her cheek to her throat and stayed there, feeling the blood pulse beneath his fingers.

"Now," she answered, surprising him.

Kyle knew he should turn and walk away, but instead he tossed his cup of coffee aside and leaned closer, feeling a pleasant twinge in his stomach. Like Macduff, he was a threat to her, cursed with the inescapable legacy of all *servi* who had dwelled in Nefandus. He might be able to kiss her there, with so many people standing around, and stop before the danger awakened inside him, but the hunger would one day become stronger than his ability to hold it back, and what would happen to her then? She had already been weakened once. Could a person die if enough of their life force were stolen from their soul? He didn't know the answer, but he felt confident that one small kiss couldn't hurt.

He kissed her temple, savoring the feel of

her hair against his face and breathing in her musk perfume. He knew better than to allow his lips to touch hers, but his mouth moved over her cheek with a will of its own, relishing her sun-warmed skin. He kissed her lightly and drew back, his face hovering inches from hers.

"I like you, Kyle," she whispered, looking up at him with sincerity. "I mean, I really like you."

His jealousy flared, not sure if she meant him or Kent. He wanted her affection to be for him alone, and yet he knew that Kent was the one she had been seeing. "I like you, too," he said, and started to kiss her again, but her hands went up between them and pushed against his chest.

"I only needed one kiss to know." She smiled.

"To know what?" He stared at her.

"I had to prove to myself that nothing would happen if I kissed you."

"And?"

"Nothing happened." She shrugged. "But I'm not ready yet. It's going to take awhile."

"We'll wait, then," he whispered, wondering if Obie could give him an incantation to control the hunger. Then Kyle remembered that Emily didn't really have a crush on him; Kent was the one she cared for. Maybe she wouldn't even like him.

The bell rang, and she started backing away. "I'll see you tomorrow," she said.

"Be ready at six. Okay? We'll get something to eat before the party." He definitely wanted to be the one who had the date with her this time, and he didn't think Kent would arrive at her house before eight.

"Sure," she answered, and walked through the metal detector.

The security guards stopped Kyle, and after they had passed the wand over his body, he sprinted down the breezeway, searching for his friends. Students rushed around him, hurrying to their classrooms. Kyle didn't see his roommates, and he debated whether to go to class. He felt too pumped with adrenaline to sit indoors. He looked out at the empty quad. He could use the time to practice. There were almost three hours before students would start bringing their lunches to the picnic tables.

Kyle found a bench at the far end of the quad and looked over the treetops. He squinted, concentrating on the image of a seagull. A long time passed and nothing happened. He was beginning to feel discouraged. Maybe the morning's episode with the birds had been only a dream that had felt real. But then, above him, dust quivered, rising in spirals, as if awaiting his command.

Soon the sky overhead became filled with seagulls soaring and falling like kites in the wind. A loud cawing startled Kyle, and he looked at the trees. The branches were lined with tattered birds, shedding plumage. Feathers blew off their bodies and whirled around the school yard.

He smiled, feeling smug, his muscles taut. More seagulls appeared, and soon the birds were jostling against each other, vying for space until the air above the quad became thick with beating wings. Birds began to fall, dissolving as they crashed down to the ground, splattering gray-green slime over the grass and leaves.

Dim and distant screams broke into Kyle's awareness, but he was in another place, far removed from school, even though his physical body still sat on the same bench. Gradually, the voices became louder. The putrid mix of vomit and sardines filled his lungs. He blinked, and when he glanced up again, the sun caught his eyes, and his last squadron of birds plummeted to the lawn, hitting the earth with soft, squishing sounds.

Panicked cries now joined the screams. Kyle glanced around. He had been focused on the gulls, his mind in a trance, and hadn't noticed the time. Now he was startled to see students crowded under the patio covering, pointing at the decaying birds. Two security guards huddled together, drenched in ectoplasm, brows furrowed. They looked confused.

"Kyle!"

Someone called his name, but he couldn't pull his eyes away from the gray-green, gelatinous mess dripping from the nearby tree branches. Slowly the heat from the sun was dissolving the sticky matter, but the rancid vapor remained. He fanned the air in front of his face.

"Why'd you do this?" Maddie cried, folding her arms over her chest. Tiny globs speckled her boots and leather jacket.

"Why would I?" Kyle felt himself sinking into the bench, trying to make himself invisible.

"We know it's you. You can't deny it now." Allison joined Maddie, scowling. Her hair had frizzed, and mascara ran in black streaks down her cheeks. One of the decomposing birds must have hit her directly on the top of the head.

"Do you think I made this mess?" Kyle stood, spreading his hands innocently.

Emily pushed her way between her friends. Ectoplasm slid down her cheek and dripped from her hair. "This was so not funny, Kyle."

"I'm sorry." He pulled off his T-shirt and handed it to her.

She began wiping the slimy droppings from her face. "I can't believe you'd do this."

"I can," Allison said and grabbed the T-shirt to wipe her neck.

But suddenly another thought occurred to

Kyle. What had happened was beyond possibility, so why were they accusing him? He wished he could pull back his apology. It was almost a confession. "What makes you think I did this?"

"Get real," Maddie said and flicked some of the foul-smelling stuff at him. It landed on his nose and slithered down to his lips. He spit, disgusted.

"You told us to come out here to see your art happening," Allison said, using her fingers to enclose the word *happening* in imaginary quotation marks. "I guess this was all a big joke to you. Ha-ha."

"You said I'd love to see what you could do with your new art form," Emily said in a mocking tone.

"I said?" Kyle felt the familiar tingle of adrenaline rush through him, and he glanced around the quad knowing Kent was near, and then he saw him at the back of the gym, dressed in jeans and a T-shirt identical to the ones Kyle wore. Kent waved before ducking between the chain-link fence and the corner of the building.

"I hope the smell goes away," Emily said

and tossed the T-shirt at Kyle. His attention came back to the three girls standing in front of him.

"Yuck! I can barely breathe," Maddie added.

"I didn't do this for the reason you think," Kyle said somberly, and something in his expression made Emily stop frowning. "What I was attempting to do failed, all right?"

Emily looked at him curiously, then nudged Maddie and grabbed Allison's arm. "Let's go," she said in a quiet voice.

The girls turned as one and started back toward the classrooms.

A few minutes later, Berto, Obie, and Samuel joined Kyle. Samuel and Obie shook their heads and burst into laughter. But Berto stared, expressionless.

"Kent told everyone he was going to do something spectacular on the quad." Samuel said grinning and holding his sides. "Everyone assumes Kent is you. Even I thought he was until I got up close enough to him to ask him what he was talking about. Why'd you make such a mess?"

"You've got one mean reputation as an artist," Obie went on. "Kent said he was going to show a living work of art, a mind-boggling happening. Everyone was excited about it and couldn't wait until lunch, but no one expected this. Is it art?"

"I guess Kent saw me practicing and decided to use it to his advantage," Kyle said unhappily, and glanced at Berto again, wondering what had upset him.

"He used it to his advantage to get everyone in the school mad at you. Just hope all the gunk dissolves before the vice-principal gets here." Obie scooped up some of the squishy stuff and examined it. "What is it, anyway?"

"Ectoplasm, I think," Kyle answered. "The residue from using my power to create things."

"This is your power?" Samuel said, staring at the mess.

Obie seemed baffled, but Berto's glare remained focused on Kyle.

"If you had gotten out here earlier, you would have seen the seagulls before they turned to mush," Kyle said defensively.

Samuel studied him. "I saw the seagulls from the classroom window. They were thick as locusts. You did that?"

Kyle nodded. "I can create things by concentrating, but so far I've only been able to make a bird appear, and not for very long." Then he caught the anxious exchange of glances between Obie and Samuel. "What now?" Kyle asked.

"Kent knows you've found your power," Samuel said. "That could be a problem."

"What's he going to do about it?" Kyle asked. "I can probably call him back more easily now."

"I don't think it's going to be that simple," Berto offered.

"Why not?" Kyle asked, feeling his heart sink.

"Because I just saw Ashley on my way out here," Berto said. "And she told me I was going to be sorry for not siding with her when I had the opportunity. What does that imply to you?"

"That she thinks Kent is going to win,"

Kyle said, but the look in Berto's eyes still bothered him. "What else is on your mind?" Kyle asked.

"Maybe you have more secrets you need to tell us about," Berto said, gazing at Kyle as if he were the enemy.

CHAPTER NINETEEN

S KYLE PARKED his car in front of Emily's house, he felt a surge of happiness he hadn't anticipated. He turned off the engine, grateful to be away from the loft and his room-mates. His nerves were still on edge from their relentless questioning. Ashley had told Berto that Kyle was keeping secrets from the other three. She found out about his mother's visit from Kent, who knew about it because of his telepathic connection to Kyle.

Kyle now regretted that he hadn't told his

friends immediately, but he hadn't been holding back the information his mother had given him so much as trying to absorb it before sharing it with the others. What his mother had said had changed everything he had thought about his life, and he was still grappling with it. He didn't know if his roommates had even believed all he had told them, but he did suspect that it was going to be a long time before they completely trusted him again, if ever. After all, he was the son of a demon. He pushed the thought aside. He wasn't going to think about it tonight.

He got out of the car and headed up the walk, glad to be outside in the cold December breeze. After everything that had happened, he was ready to party. He ran up the porch steps and rang the bell.

The door flew open, as if someone in the house had been waiting for him. Emily's eight-year-old brother stuck his head outside, his golden curls a halo around his chubby face. "Emmy said to go away."

A smaller boy ducked under the older one's

arm. "She never wants to see you again." He stuck out his tongue.

Kyle bent down. "How do you know I'm the guy she meant? Maybe I'm the one she wants to see," he teased.

The two boys looked at each other. Then the older one rammed the door against the wall, leaving it wide open. "Emmy, is he the one you want to see or the one you don't want to see?"

"Kyle!" Emily said, and swallowed something in her mouth. She looked stricken. She bolted up from the couch, brown candy-wrappers scattering around her, and stood trapped between a coffee table, the sofa, and the Christmas tree. She wore a tattered bathrobe and clutched a half gallon of ice cream in the crook of her arm. "I didn't think you'd be coming by after . . ." her words fell away.

"After what?" he asked, pushing his way around the boys and stepping inside. He hoped she wasn't going to change her mind about going to the party, but she definitely didn't look happy to see him.

"Did something happen?" he asked. He didn't have to be a mind reader to know she'd had another difficult encounter with Kent.

"You mean in the last hour?" She licked at the chocolate on her lips and made a face he didn't understand. Was it one of exasperation or sadness?

He felt angry with himself. He should have known that Kent would visit Emily that day and try to wreck his plans. "Look, I apologize for anything I might have said or done. I haven't been myself lately, but I want to go to the party with you. Get dressed. . . . Please."

He felt foolish and stopped pleading with her. He sounded like the singer in one of those lovesick cowboy songs, begging his girl to come back to him.

She sighed. "Sometimes you seem so sweet, and other times . . ." She handed her brothers the container of ice cream. "All right, I'll go, but we won't have time to get something to eat first. It's going to take me a while to get ready; I have to wash my hair."

Three noisy cartoon shows later, Kyle

heard footsteps and went into the foyer. Emily came down the stairs, wearing a low-slung chiffon skirt and a cropped top, her hair soft on her shoulders.

"Wow," Kyle said, overcome. "You look great."

"Thanks." She smiled self-consciously as he guided her outside.

At the car she looked up at him. "I wanted to go to the party, but I figured you wouldn't come back." Her breath was sweet as it mingled with his. He had the urge to kiss her, but she seemed to sense his thoughts and shifted away from him.

He opened the car door. She started to climb in, but something made her stop and look behind her. Fear shimmered in her eyes.

"What?" he asked.

She shrugged. "I just had the weirdest feeling that someone was watching us."

Kyle turned and studied the shadows moving beneath the trees. A soft whisper filled the night. Was it only the breeze rustling through the leaves, or was Kent there, hiding in the dark, taunting him and waiting for a chance to attack? A terrible heaviness came over Kyle, and his muscles tightened in alarm. He should have been more careful.

He tried to recall his mother's exact words. She had told him that Kent had become self-aware and was trying to give himself the breath of life. But did that mean he had to steal it from another person, like Emily? Kyle glanced at Emily, suddenly afraid for her. He needed to protect her.

"Get in," he ordered.

"Why are you in such a hurry now?" she asked good-naturedly; then she caught the look in his eyes and got in, snapping the seat belt into place. "What's wrong?"

"We didn't go to dinner, so I want to get to the party before all the chips are gone," Kyle said, trying to be funny, but the words hung awkwardly in the air. He slammed the passenger-side door and tried to shake off his fear as he ran around the car and jumped in behind the steering wheel. He turned the key in the ignition and jammed his foot on the accelerator.

The car roared away, fishtailing wildly.

"Kyle?" Emily said and touched his shoulder. "Slow down. I'll buy you some chips if they're all gone."

He caught her smile, but in the dim light cast by the streetlamps she looked uneasy, as if she had also sensed something in her front yard that shouldn't logically have been there.

A few blocks later, Kyle turned down a street already crowded with parked cars. Kids had come to Maddie's party early, excited to begin the winter holiday. Some mingled on the front porch, and a group of guys were playing touch football on the front lawn.

Kyle parked and got out. The music boomed like distant thunder, and the steady beat broke through his tension. He helped Emily from the car, then kissed her cheek and wrapped his arm around her, enjoying the softness of her body against his as they walked toward the party.

Girls in slinky tops and short skirts danced on the driveway, singing the lyrics to the song. Kyle started moving with the beat. Emily leaned into him, swaying sensually. He looked down at her and kissed the back of her neck. He loved the dreamy feel of the night; then sadness swept his joy away. Where could their relationship go? Even if she did like him and not Kent, what then? This wasn't the normal situation, where they could see each other every day at school and kiss in the hallways like other couples. What would happen if they actually fell in love? He was immortal, and cursed with a hunger that would eventually drive him to destroy her.

He stopped dancing, and when he did, Emily spun around.

"What's wrong?" she asked, but before he could answer, her mouth opened, freeing a scream. She stepped back, struggling to pull him with her.

Kyle started to turn, afraid to see what had frightened her. Something huge hit his back and he fell forward, slamming his face into the grass and skidding across the lawn into unconsciousness.

CHAPTER TWENTY

A THICK SOUND started up Kyle's throat, and then he realized he was moaning from the pain shooting up his spine. He spit out mud and grass and started to panic. His lungs felt as if they were on fire, and his nose was too clogged to pull in enough air to breathe. He opened his mouth, and slowly the normal rise and fall of his chest resumed. He rolled over, expecting to see Kent. Instead, a circle of kids from the party looked down at him, a mixture of revulsion and concern on their faces.

"Kyle said he was going to show us a defensive move," Barry insisted, trying to explain to the crowd what had happened. "He wanted us to tackle him when his back was turned."

"Right," Maddie answered sarcastically. "Everyone asks for that kind of torture."

"I swear on my football scholarship: he asked us to blindside him," Sledge said to Maddie, while offering his hand to Kyle. "Are you all right?" His concern seemed genuine.

Kyle nodded as he gripped Sledge's hand and let Sledge pull him to his feet. His legs felt wobbly, his head pounded, and he wasn't sure he'd ever feel normal again. He gingerly touched the warm liquid on his face and knew his nose was bleeding.

"I can't believe you guys would tackle him like that." Emily placed her arms protectively around Kyle's waist, apparently afraid he'd lose his balance and fall again.

"I bet his nose is broken," Maddie said. "It looks smashed. Maybe we should take him to the hospital."

"It's okay," Kyle said, his eyes still watering from his collision with the ground. "I just need to wash my face."

"I apologize for my maniac brother and his gruesome friend," Maddie said and gave Sledge a cold look. "This isn't the first party I've given that he's tried to ruin."

"Sledge is telling the truth," Kyle said. There was no doubt in his mind that Kent had set him up for the bone-crushing tackle. He gazed beyond the kids gathered around him, convinced he would see Kent lurking somewhere in the dark, laughing at what had happened. "I asked him to tackle me."

"I told you." Sledge picked up his football, suddenly uninterested in Kyle. Barry charged across the lawn to receive the pass.

"Let's go inside," Emily said to Kyle. "You need to put something on your nose to stop the swelling."

Drops of Kyle's blood spilled onto the polished tile floor. Kids stopped dancing and parted, staring squeamishly at the tiny rivulets running from his nose and dripping off his chin. This was not the evening with Emily that Kyle had planned.

Alone in the bathroom, he stared at his

reflection in the mirror, feeling glum in spite of the laughter and music coming from the other side of the door. He pressed a washcloth over his nose, and when the bleeding stopped, he cleaned his face and then scrubbed at the stains on his shirt.

His head was still throbbing when he went back to the party. Emily was dancing with Tinesa and Zack. Kyle watched for a moment, then wandered out to the backyard, found an ice chest filled with soft drinks, grabbed two cans of lemon-lime soda, and pressed one to either side of his nose. When the pain subsided, he went back inside.

Tinesa and Zack were still dancing, but Emily was no longer with them.

"Where did Emily go?" Kyle asked.

"She just left with you." Tinesa tilted her head and gave him a curious look. "Why did you put the bloody shirt back on?"

"Which way did Emily go?" Kyle asked, realizing at once that she had left with Kent.

"What are you on, man?" Zack asked. "You just took her out the front door. You should know where she is."

Kyle spun away from them and sprinted outside, across the porch. He jumped onto the lawn, tossing the two drinks aside. The tab on one popped open, and the can shot around like a rocket, spraying carbonated soda on everyone in the yard. Kids screamed and a guy cursed.

Kyle ignored them and looked both ways down the street. When he didn't see Emily and Kent, he hurried over to Sledge and Barry at the far end of the yard.

"Did you see Emily?" he asked Sledge.

Sledge narrowed his eyes and studied Kyle as if he thought it were a trick question. "She was with you. You just crossed the street with her."

Barry stared at Kyle inquisitively. "Your nose is swollen. Did you hit it again?"

"Which way did I take Emily?" Kyle asked with rising frustration.

"Man, you need to see a doctor. I think you've got a concussion." Barry tossed the football aside. "Come on, we'll drive you to the hospital."

Kyle couldn't bear the thought that something might happen to Emily because of his carelessness. "Just tell me which way we went."

"That way." Barry pointed with his thumb.

Kyle took off down the block. At the corner, he saw Kent and Emily on the other side of the street, leaning against a palm tree, kissing.

"Stop! That's my kiss!" he yelled, instantly wishing he could pull his words back. How asinine had that sounded? Maybe he did have a concussion, after all.

He glanced back over his shoulder, hoping no one had heard him, but already kids on the drive had stopped dancing and were watching him. He dodged across the street, grabbed Kent's arm and yanked him away from Emily.

"What are you doing?" Kyle asked.

"I'm having the fun you should be having, bro." Kent grinned wickedly and fondled Emily's shoulder. His hand slipped down her back to her waist and pulled her close to him.

Emily gasped and looked from one to the other. "I can't believe it," she said. "You're twins. No wonder you seem so nice one minute and so—"

"Didn't you notice his nose?" Kyle complained angrily, still jealous that Kent had kissed her.

"He said the bleeding made it look worse than it was," Emily said, with a mix of anger and shock. "Forget about the nose. Why didn't you tell me there were two of you?"

"You don't have an answer for that one, do you, Kylie?" Kent smirked as if he were enjoying it all.

Kyle glared at him. "Please give me a few minutes alone with my brother, Emily."

"Like you needed to ask," Emily said. "I hope you guys have had lots of fun comparing notes, because I never want to see either of you again. Go find some other victim for your stupid pranks." She turned and walked away, but not before Kyle saw the hurt in her eyes.

"Emily." Kyle started after her, but Kent caught him and pulled him back.

"Kylie-Kyle-Kyle, what's wrong with you?" Kent asked. "You're living a completely mundane life, worrying about Emily, and gas bills, and getting good grades, when you could be thriving on the other side. You're immortal, the son of a blessed demon. Do you even know how much fun you're missing?"

Kyle paused. Was Kent trying to distract him from what he needed to do, or was there—

"Truth in what I'm saying?" Kent flashed a smile, his telepathic hold incredibly strong. "You belong on the other side." Kent put a brotherly arm around Kyle. "Go there with me now, and we'll end this conflict. Nefandus is big enough for both of us. It's our home."

Kyle stared at Kent. For the first time, he felt uncertain. Was it possible that Nefandus really was where he belonged? "No." Kyle shook his head, resolute. "I despise you."

"But I am you," Kent whispered. "You're trying to suppress your true nature. We always hate in other people the very traits we try to deny that we ourselves possess. That's a fact."

"You're not me. I made you up," Kyle said at last. "You don't exist."

"But from what did you create me? I know you want to absorb me, but what happens to

Kylie if you do? You won't be the perfect responsible person—"

"I'm not that now," Kyle argued.

"Are you talking about your bad-boy reputation?" Kent taunted, making Kyle feel suddenly childish.

"I struggle," Kyle said, hating the whine in his voice. The hunger was always waiting near the surface and hard to fight.

"You hold yourself in," Kent went on. "I'm everything you don't want to own up to. If you take me back, what happens? You'll have more evil inside you, and then what becomes of sweet Emily?"

Kyle shuddered, wondering if there was truth in what Kent was saying.

"Do you think she'd be happy living in Nefandus?" Kent continued.

"No," Kyle said, and his voice sounded faraway and hollow.

"I know everything about you," Kent answered. "You created me from your thoughts, and all of that energy is still inside me, connected to desires you keep hidden even from yourself. Don't you ever stop running and just think? If you did, you'd know I'm telling you the truth."

"You're a *tulpa*," Kyle answered. "And I'm going to call back your existence."

"But not before I destroy Emily," Kent answered threateningly.

Kyle slammed his fist into Kent's face, then stepped back, holding his knuckles. The pain was unbearable. He'd probably broken one or two fingers; even worse was the smirk creeping over Kent's lips, Kyle's reaction seemed exactly the one he had hoped to provoke.

In that moment, Kyle realized that Kent's taunting had been an attempt to distract him from what he needed to do. It had worked. He had wasted too much time already. He stared at Kent, determined to absorb him. He tried to envision Kent gone, but the process baffled him. He should have thought it through before then. It was easy to imagine something; he daydreamed all the time. But to absorb a thought and make it vanish was difficult, maybe even impossible. How did one do that? He squinted, trying to imagine empty space where Kent now stood. Nothing happened.

Kent roared with laughter. "You don't have a clue. Let me explain the *tulpa* rules. Rule number one, you let them create you, and rule number two, you never, ever let them *un*create you, because life is way too freaking cool!"

"I'll destroy you," Kyle said, with rising determination. "It's only a matter of time."

"You think?" Kent answered, with cocky confidence. "I'm the one who deserves this life, because I'm the one willing to live it. You just wander around, waiting for the next catastrophe. You waste hours, entire days." Kent threw his hands up in frustration. "I've tried to warn you that you're letting something precious slip away, but you're too dense to understand. It's too late for you, anyway. No one can withstand the black diamond."

Kent stuck his hand into his pocket and pulled out the gem. It caught the light from the street, and its facets sent out brilliant sparks.

Kyle stared at its blinding intensity. The

diamond, even though it was black, looked like a tiny sun resting in Kent's palm.

"Soon I'll be the master," Kent whispered with dark resolve. "Then there will be only one of us: the right one, me."

CHAPTER TWENTY-ONE

"**B**UT WHY DIDN'T Kent use the diamond against you when he had the chance?" Samuel asked, popping open a can of cola. "All he had to do was make a wish."

"I'm not sure it's that simple," Kyle answered. "Kent seemed confident, but then he turned and walked away. So maybe he hasn't figured out how to use it yet."

Kyle stood over the kitchen sink and swallowed two aspirin. Then he grabbed a bag of frozen peas from the freezer and held it over his throbbing nose. He straddled a chair at the table and stuck his bruised fingers into a bowl of ice water. Berto, Obie, and Samuel watched him. They had been about to leave for Maddie's when he had returned to the loft.

"You don't have to endure the pain," Obie said. "I've fixed worse wounds."

"What if something goes wrong?" Kyle asked, afraid the incantation might make the soreness worse.

"Trust me." Obie marked the air, and letters swept toward Kyle, twisting and turning into thin threads that bored into the skin.

Kyle clenched his teeth, expecting at least a twinge of discomfort, but he felt nothing, and the aching ended.

"Wow." Kyle touched his nose, amazed; even the swelling was gone. He stretched his fingers. "Thanks." He dropped the bag of peas onto the table.

"If Kent had the diamond," Berto said, going back to the original conversation, "and didn't use it, then maybe he has another plan, one that involves more than just destroying Kyle."

"Or Kent could be afraid," Obie suggested. "Magicians put curses on strong charms. That way, if it falls into the wrong hands, the magic is still protected."

"Could the diamond need a particular alignment of stars in order to work?" Kyle asked, remembering the mural on Kent's bedroom walls. "That would explain why Kent was spending so much time with Ashley, looking at astrological charts."

"I bet there's a clue hidden somewhere in the mural," Obie said. "We should go over there now."

Kyle started to get up, but then he glanced at the clock. It was nine-thirty. "Maybe we should wait until morning. Mrs. Caine goes to bed early."

"I think we'd better go now," Berto said, grabbing the car keys and tossing them to Kyle. "You said Kent lives with her; if we wait until tomorrow, he'll probably be there. Right now he's most likely out partying."

Kyle thought of Emily and hoped she was all right.

"Let's go," Samuel said, kicking back his

chair. The four of them started toward the door. On the way, Obie grabbed the book on Tibetan doctrines.

"Maybe I can find something on absorbing *tulpas* that we haven't read before," Obie said, thumbing through the pages as they hurried outside.

Kyle grabbed his jacket and slipped it on, although he didn't think the cold he was feeling came from the weather.

Soon Kyle's car was speeding down the freeway, the tailpipe trailing black exhaust. A tense silence settled over the four of them, and Kyle wondered if his roommates felt as he did— that time was running out.

Maybe together he and his friends really were the Four of Legend, but Kyle had always imagined that the Four would be like avenging seraphs, with black spreading wings—not ordinary-looking guys who had trouble paying their rent.

They may have had powers, but there was nothing miraculous about their lives. He didn't feel like a hero who could storm into Nefandus, free the *servi*, seal the portals, and still survive. But if he and his friends truly were the Four, then why hadn't the Dark Goddess come to help them? They desperately needed a guide. They didn't even know the lore surrounding the black diamond. They knew only that they were supposed to take it with them when they returned to Nefandus on their final quest. Why was that so important?

A sudden flare of brake lights brought his attention back to driving. The traffic was knotted, and horns blared. Kyle exited the freeway and raced through the surface streets, dodging around slower cars. As he turned down the block where Mrs. Caine lived, his stomach tensed with unexpected nervousness. Kyle wondered if the others felt the change in the atmosphere as they neared the house.

Berto looked pale in the reflection from the green dashboard lights. His eyes showed vigilance.

"What is it?" Kyle whispered.

Berto shook his head. "I don't know. Something weird."

"The lights are on," Obie said from the back, his voice strained. "Maybe Kent is home after all."

"If he is, then I think he's learned how to use the diamond." Kyle turned off the ignition and put on the brake. "And he's waiting for us."

CHAPTER TWENTY-TWO

KYLE STEPPED ACROSS the porch, his roommates close behind him. Loud music came from the house, it sounded as if a party were going on. He started to knock, then paused as he glanced through the front window. Between the branches and tinsel of the Christmas tree, he caught glimpses of Mrs. Caine and Kent. He stared blankly, unable to comprehend what he saw. "What's he doing to her?"

"I don't know," Obie said.

Kyle leaned closer, trying to see beyond the

blinking holiday lights. His breath fogged the cold glass pane, and he wiped at it with his sleeve. Mrs. Caine was struggling with Kent, trying to take something from his hand.

"Maybe they're fighting over the diamond," Samuel said.

Kyle rapped on the window, and then tried the doorknob. "It's locked." His mouth went dry with sudden fear, and he pounded on the wood until his knuckles hurt. "Mrs. Caine, open the door."

Crashing sounds came from inside. Kyle peered through the window again. A lamp had toppled, and the light made shadows fall diagonally across the wall, giving a crooked, haunted look to the room.

Kent jerked away from Mrs. Caine and headed toward the kitchen. She ran clumsily after him and grabbed his arm, then thrashed about, losing a slipper as she tried to pry something from his fingers. Kent spun around, attempting to free himself from her. She lost her balance and fell over the record player, toppling it. The music stopped. An eerie silence followed, and the soft sobs of Mrs. Caine's weeping filled the lull.

Kyle stepped back and lunged at the door, aiming with his shoulder as he had seen people do in movies.

"Stop," Samuel yelled; he tried to grab him. Kyle slipped through his hands and slammed into the wood. The hinges rattled, but the lock didn't give. Kyle staggered back, moaning. Pain ripped through his shoulder.

Berto laughed and shook his head. "What were you thinking?"

Obie marked the runic inscription for *fire-start* in front of them.

"Obie's spell-casting didn't work the last time we were here," Kyle said, making an excuse for his brainless plan.

"I couldn't counteract the hex," Obie argued, flinging the incantation for *fire-start* at the entrance, and quickly following it up with another. Flames flared around the frame, dripping small fires to the porch. The door burst inward, falling to the ground with a loud boom.

Kyle raced inside to where Mrs. Caine lay, sprawled helplessly near the coffee table. She didn't appear happy or relieved to see him. Instead she frowned.

Kent paused in the entrance to the kitchen, his hand on the swinging door, and looked back, seeming astonished, but excited as well. "I didn't think you'd come to visit me so soon," he said, and stepped back into the living room.

"I thought he'd be more disappointed to see us," Samuel said to his roommates, slowly approaching Kent, with Berto and Obie on either side of him.

"He was last time," Kyle answered; he hoped Kent's running from him earlier that night hadn't been a ploy to lure all four of them to the house. Maybe Kent wanted to capture them and turn them over to the authorities in Nefandus for a reward.

Kyle helped Mrs. Caine stand. He brushed a few strands of hair from her eyes and knew something was wrong. She was no longer the sweet-looking woman from his childhood. Her gaze seemed distant, her face haggard, and heavy, dark circles lined her eyes, as if worry had kept her awake night after night.

"Don't mind about me," she said forcefully, her icy fingers digging into his wrist. "Get the diamond. He's going to use it against you."

"Don't worry," Kyle said trying to sound confident. "I know how to defeat him now."

But Mrs. Caine didn't give him a reassuring look, only one of terrible regret. "I tried to stop him," she went on, evidently blaming herself. "I should have, but I'm not as strong as I once was. I'm losing energy."

Kyle had the impression that there was more meaning in what she was saying than the words conveyed, but the significance was lost on him.

"What do you mean?" he asked, wishing that for once she'd divulge all her secrets.

"The only thing you can do now is leave," she said, breaking eye contact with him. "Get out while you can."

"I won't leave you," he answered. But he didn't see any gratitude reflected in her eyes. And then he smelled something beneath the aroma of the pine tree—the citrus scent he remembered from his childhood. Could the fragrance have come from Mrs. Caine's perfume and not his nightmares?

"You'd better do something," Samuel said. He touched the stone totems hanging around his neck.

Berto, Samuel, and Obie had encircled Kent, penning him in.

"We're waiting for you," Berto said, and he blocked Kent as Kent tried to dodge around him.

Kyle pushed Mrs. Caine behind him. His jaw muscles twitched as he imagined Kent disintegrating, and then, without warning, part of him seemed to travel to another place, and the link between him and his twin felt stronger than mere telepathy. They were bound together as one. Kyle felt certain of success now, and he stared at Kent, imagining him gone.

Kent brought his hands up to his head, as if to deflect Kyle's thoughts. He shuddered and closed his eyes, apparently in pain, letting his fingers splay over his face.

Seconds ticked by. The connection between the two became more powerful, but Kent didn't fade. Kyle tried again, anger and frustration now fueling his hatred. A strange dizziness made him sway, and his muscles ached, as if he were coming down with flu.

Kent's eyes flashed open. "You don't know how to absorb me, do you?" He stared at Kyle, dumbfounded, his fear turning to triumph.

"What's wrong?" Samuel asked. "He should be gone. You were concentrating so hard even I could feel your hostility."

"The room was buzzing with your hatred," Berto agreed.

"Just unthink him," Obie ordered.

"I tried," Kyle said with rising irritation. "What does the book say to do? There must be some ritual I need to perform."

"The book isn't a manual. It doesn't give steps, because I doubt many people have run into this problem before." Obie ran his finger down a page. "It says it can take up to three weeks of intense concentration to absorb a *tulpa*."

Kyle grabbed the book from Obie and threw it at the wall. The binding broke, and pages fluttered around the room. "What if you only have three minutes?"

"I'll give you a moment to regret your failings," Kent said and placed the diamond in the center of his palm.

Berto tried to grab it, but Kent moved more quickly. He closed his hand around the gem, then grinned in victory and opened his fist, uncurling his fingers slowly. The diamond pulsed with blinding brightness.

Kyle stepped closer, drawn to its mesmerizing radiance. A dreamy feeling came over him, igniting an unexpected desire. He didn't understand the craving; he only knew he wanted to join the light.

"What are you doing?" Samuel grabbed Kyle's arm and pulled him back.

Kyle heard someone whining, and then he realized the sound was coming from his own throat. He stared at Samuel, resentful, and longing to be united with the diamond's light. He didn't understand his feelings. After all, the diamond would destroy him, yet, more than anything, Kyle wanted to fade into the gem's luster and become one with it.

"We need to try something else," Berto said, slapping Kyle in the face to break his trance.

Suddenly, Obie threw back his head; he let out a cry and lunged forward, as he must have done centuries back, charging into battle with his tribe of Visigoth warriors. His right hand slashed the air, but instead of holding a sword, he wrote runic inscriptions. The room hummed with magic, and the smell of burning roses became overpowering.

The letters flared and whipped around Kent, spreading over his face and slithering in an endless pattern across his skin. He screamed in rage, but before he could fight back, Obie cast another spell.

This time, Kent dove behind the couch. The chain of interlocking words smashed into the upholstery, and the plaid fabric smoldered. Silence followed.

"Is he gone?" Samuel asked.

As if in answer, Kent stood and stepped from behind the couch, his face dead calm.

"Something's different," Berto said. "He's changed."

Kent stared at them with dark resolve, waiting.

"What now?" Kyle asked.

Obie didn't answer. He stepped forward, his fingers working rapidly. Kyle recognized the stunning spell.

A halo blazed around Obie as his power continued to build, and then he pitched the spell. Kent didn't move. He stared at the burning letters and, at the last possible moment, held the diamond up and caught Obie's magic inside the gem and deflected it. The inscription turned and flew back at Obie with lightning speed. It struck his chest, and the impact catapulted him backward. He hit a maple hutch with a loud thud. The dishes inside rattled and crashed as Obie slumped to the floor.

Kyle, Samuel, and Berto rushed to kneel beside him.

"Are you all right?" Kyle asked.

Obie regained consciousness and blinked rapidly. "What was that?"

"Kent used the diamond to boomerang your spell and cast it back at you," Kyle explained.

"I must be good." Obie tried to grin, but his smile turned to a grimace. "Because it hurts like hell."

Then, without warning, hot pain made Kyle cough and sputter. He tried to clear his throat. For a moment he couldn't draw in air, and after that, he felt a strange lightness in the chest.

"What now?" Berto asked.

Kyle shook his head. "I don't know. I couldn't breathe for a moment."

From across the room, another cough made them turn. Kent wheezed and exhaled. He took in deep, crackling breaths, as if his lungs were paper dry from disuse and needed exercise before they could function on their own.

"He just took his first breath," Kyle said. Then, remembering his mother's warning, he added, "We have to stop him before his heart beats."

Kent pressed his hand on his breastbone, visibly trembling with excitement. His fingers probed around his ribs, apparently searching for a gentle thud of heart muscle. His smiled faded, and he turned, looking at them with cruel determination.

Mrs. Caine scrambled over to Kyle, scraping against the Christmas tree's branches and knocking off an ornament. She looked directly into Kyle's eyes. "When your heart stops beating," she said, "then his begins."

CHAPTER TWENTY-THREE

IN THE TINT OF red and green Christmas lights, Mrs. Caine looked drawn and defeated, her eyes bloodshot and watery. Kyle placed his arm around her and realized she was shivering violently. Everything she had seen that night must have been affecting her. He feared she was going into shock and needed to go to the hospital. He pulled off his jacket and placed it over her shoulders.

"I'm sorry you had to see all of this," Kyle

said. "It will be over soon. Maybe you can help. What else do you know about Kent?"

"We're running out of time," Berto warned. He and Samuel stood, dragging Obie with them.

Kyle looked up and froze. Kent held the diamond between his index finger and thumb. The gem's fiery radiance burst through the room. Kyle pulled his gaze away, but afterimages burned his vision. He took hold of Mrs. Caine and helped her stand. Together they edged back across the living room, away from Kent.

"Actions have consequences," Kent said, stalking after them. "You can't create another living human being to soothe your own loneliness and then discard him when you find other friends."

A thin vapor uncurled from the jewel, snaking toward Kyle.

"I gave you a chance," Kent went on. "Just remember that. I was better than you. I offered you the opportunity to be real brothers."

The mist split into four sinuous tendrils, one winding toward each Son.

"You don't have to make it easy for him," Berto said and grabbed Kyle's belt, yanking him back with the others.

Kyle had been unaware that he was standing immobile, basking in the diamond's light.

"Kent wants his revenge," Obie said, his voice breaking through Kyle's daze. "Hatred is driving him. Maybe we can find a way to use that to our advantage."

"Hatred," Kyle whispered, and suddenly he remembered his mother's words: *hatred cannot be conquered by hatred, but by love alone is destroyed.* He started to make the connection with Kent again, but the diamond flashed and drew his eyes back to it.

"What did you say?" Samuel asked.

But it was too late. Kyle couldn't quite remember what he had been thinking; he was aware only of the diamond's dangerous beauty. Its vapors slithered around him in a gentle caress, tickling his nostrils and filling his lungs, their toxins slipping into his blood and pulsing through his veins to his heart. Already he felt himself descending into another world, lethargy taking hold. He was vaguely aware of Samuel pushing in front of him.

"I think we were too hasty in coming here," Samuel said, his voice distant and echoing. "We didn't think it through."

Samuel touched the totem hanging around his neck and found the stone emblem of the coyote. Immediately the air above them bulged with what looked like the outline of a dog curled up and sleeping. The shape became dense with prickles of gray and brown fur, and then the coyote fell to the floor in front of them with a loud thump.

Kent took a quick step back, startled by the sight of the beast materializing at his feet. The vapors from the diamond spread out in a dusty haze before falling to the ground as pink ash. Kent stared scornfully at the scrawny beast.

The coyote mewled, then stood on shaky forelegs, chuffing and snorting, trying to get its bearings. It wobbled forward, dried leaves falling from its fur, and nudged Samuel's leg with its muzzle.

"You've got to be kidding," Kent said

derisively. "You're one of the Four. I thought you'd call forth the hound of hell. This creature is all mangy fur and bone."

The coyote raised its head and growled at Kent.

"That's okay, boy," Samuel said, rubbing behind its ears. "You're just learning, like the rest of us."

"All those stories about the Legend," Kent went on, a quizzical expression on his face. "Why is everyone in Nefandus so afraid of the four of you?"

"They're afraid of us?" Kyle asked as he exchanged bewildered glances with his friends.

"We've got to go back to Nefandus," Obie said. "And visit the library. What do you think they've written about us?"

"Let's just hope we survive this evening, so we can find out," Kyle said, edging back. He guided Mrs. Caine behind the couch as Kent started to aim the diamond at them again.

Without warning, the coyote crouched and then leaped recklessly at Kent. Its forepaws pounded his chest, surprising him. Kent staggered back, tripping over the fallen lamp, and lost his balance. He fell straight backward.

The coyote landed on top of him, snarling. Kent grabbed its neck and threw the animal aside. The beast let out a startled yelp and hit the floor, skidding into the wall. It lay still; then its brown eyes opened and it bared its teeth in what looked like a wicked grin. After that, its snout pointed down to the black diamond jammed between its paws.

CHAPTER TWENTY-FOUR

"**N**O!" KENT YELLED, and stepped back, his arms thrashing wildly as he attempted to turn and run; but Kyle had already started to absorb him. The connection was strong, and the energy linking them was filled with compassion this time.

Kent lifted one leg clumsily and dropped it. His heels scraping the carpet as he shuffled backward, dragging his feet like heavy weights. "You can't destroy me," he said, plaintively.

"I'm not," Kyle answered, calmly pressing

forward. "You're becoming part of me." In his mind, Kyle reverently repeated the words his mother had given him, as if praying: *hatred cannot be conquered by hatred, but by love alone is destroyed.*

Kent let out a horrible yell, his mouth twisting in pain, as his body began to blur.

"I'm sorry," Kyle whispered, knowing Kent must have had some awareness of his own existence and that it must have been terrifying for him to know his life was about to end.

As Kent became transparent, Kyle risked a glance behind the couch. He was worried about Mrs. Caine, but nothing could have prepared him for what he saw. He fell to his knees. What had happened? Something was terribly wrong. His concentration stopped, and his bond with Kent was shattered.

Mrs. Caine was fading. Her ghostly image stared sadly back at him. She waved her nearly invisible hands, motioning for him to turn his attention back to Kent. When he didn't, her mouth moved silently, as if she were desperate to tell him something.

Kent stomped toward Kyle, his body robust

and solid again. "Now you see the price you'll have to pay if you destroy me. Are you strong enough to do that?"

Berto helped Kyle stand up. "You can't let him use Mrs. Caine as a hostage."

"Are you telling me her life is bound to his?" Kyle said, feeling overwhelmed.

"Apparently so," Obie said, his hand poised to cast a spell even though none had worked before. "He knows you'd never do anything to harm her."

"I can't absorb Kent if it means destroying Mrs. Caine." Kyle felt a terrible hollowness in his stomach.

"But you must." Mrs. Caine stood, becoming visible as she spoke. She walked unsteadily toward him. "You have to face your destiny."

Growling suddenly interrupted their conversation. A series of yelps was followed by a loud thud. Kyle whipped around. Samuel lay slumped on the floor. The coyote licked his head, whining. Kent stood over them, grinning maliciously, holding the diamond. Obie and Berto ran to Samuel.

"I've failed everyone now," Kyle said to Mrs. Caine. "But I couldn't let him harm you."

"Don't you understand?" Mrs. Caine scolded weakly. "You don't have a choice."

Kent smirked. "Why waste time explaining things to him, when his existence is going to end so soon?" He spun the diamond on his palm. "I think I'll destroy the Four of Legend and become the king hell-raiser of Nefandus. Whom should I take out first?"

Light pulsed around the jewel and then shot at Kyle.

"Come freely," Kent said in a silken voice, "and I'll protect Mrs. Caine."

Kyle nodded and took a step. The diamond's radiance gripped him with a physical force, tugging at him like an undertow in the ocean. His body swayed, and his stomach reeled as bile rose in his throat. He swallowed hard to quell the nausea and tottered forward, seeking the light.

Berto wrestled Kyle back and restrained him. "Don't give in to Kent. We'll figure out a way to stop him."

"I've won," Kent countered with cocky assurance, and then he asked Kyle, "Why are you hesitating? Inside the light is where you want to be, isn't it?"

Kyle nodded, his mind already adrift. He gazed into the brilliance, welcoming its caress. It flowed into him gently, and then, without warning, a painful jolt made him cry out. Something inside him had snapped. He became weightless and drifted up.

At first he thought he had turned to shadow, but when he looked down, he saw a ghost image of himself rising from his body through the top of his head. He was unable to resist the entity pulling his spirit forward.

A fanfare of blinding lights exploded around him, as if he were in the middle of an eerie firestorm. He must have been imprisoned in the center of the diamond. He sensed the presence of another, and then a shape roared from the brightness, forming a woman of dangerous beauty, her long hair curled in flashing flames behind her as she swept toward him. He recognized her from Kent's mural.

"Who are you?" Kyle asked. But without a body his voice was no more than a gust of wind.

With a rasp of metal, the woman unsheathed a sword, and focused her aim on his abdomen. She lifted the heavy blade and swung. It whisked through the air with the crack of a whip. Kyle tried to run, but his spirit only waggled and bobbed. The sharp blade barely missed him.

The woman brushed her hand through the air, trying to grasp something in front of Kyle. Then he glanced down and saw her target; a wispy cord attached to his chest. The spiderweb thread was the only thing connecting him to his body. Once it was severed, his heart would stop beating, and Kent's would start.

The woman stood over him, an evil glimmer in her warrior eyes. She lifted the sword. Kyle bowed his head and prayed, aware of the slowing thud of his heartbeat in a body far away. He couldn't die, but once the cord was severed, would his spirit drift for eternity in this hellish light while his body stood frozen in Mrs. Caine's living room?

CHAPTER TWENTY-FIVE

THE SWORD CAME down with fiery force, red embers sparking from the blade. A sudden breeze caught the cord and rolled it upward, lifting Kyle's ghost image with it. The razor's edge sliced only air. The woman spun around, searching for the wind's source, then took a warrior's stance, her skirt billowing, as she challenged her foe.

Kyle looked into the blinding light following the woman's gaze. Berto's dream-walking spirit floated forward, fanning the air and making Kyle's tether to life flutter wildly.

"Berto, watch out," Kyle tried to yell, but his words came out a dry whistle.

The woman lunged forward, thrusting the blade at Berto. The steel caught the light, reflecting a kaleidoscope of rainbows. Berto dodged her attack and sped over to Kyle.

"How did you get inside the diamond?" Kyle asked.

"You're on an astral plane," Berto answered. "I saw the silver cord leaving your body, so I left mine and followed the thread."

"Who is the woman?" Kyle nervously watched her.

"Our sworn enemy," Berto answered. "Just think of her as another class of Regulator guarding the astral planes so we can't sneak into Nefandus that way."

The woman stalked toward them, sword poised at one side, ready to swing. Alarm shot through Kyle as she charged again. The blade came down, but before it nicked the cord, Berto yanked Kyle away, and then they fell backward, spiraling down and back into life.

Kyle slammed into his body with a painful jolt, the woman's ear-piercing scream following after him. Obie and Samuel looked up and grabbed him as he started to fall. His body ached and throbbed. He feared he was going to pass out. His heart loped oddly, skipping beats, and then, at last, the normal rhythm returned as his spirit readjusted itself to the confinement of flesh and bone.

Kent looked up, livid, and quickly realigned the diamond's light to point toward Kyle's eyes.

"Try once more," Mrs. Caine encouraged Kyle. "He won't be satisfied to have just your life. You saw the mural. He wants to lead the armies of Nefandus into the earth realm. Grant me this one last wish. Destroy him."

Even as she spoke, Kyle imagined a bridge linking him with his twin. In his mind he gently guided Kent home.

"No," Kent shouted hysterically, his expression one of horror. A nimbus flickered around him, and then he became colorless, a writing outline of himself, before he disappeared. A curious sensation rippled through Kyle, and he knew Kent had settled into his unconscious mind again, down in the deep waters where dreams were spawned.

"Are you all right?" Berto asked.

Kyle nodded, but as he turned his attention to Mrs. Caine, the ground began to shake. The vibration worked its way up his legs and through his back.

"Is it an earthquake?" Berto asked, bracing himself against the wall. "I think the house is going to collapse."

The floorboards buckled and broke as the tremors continued. Splintered wood tore through the carpeting, jutting out at dangerous angles. The picture frames banged against the wall, and then the lights went out in the living room.

"Where's Mrs. Caine?" Kyle shouted, hoping somehow she had survived. He stepped into the falling debris trying to see her through the plaster raining down around them. Someone grabbed his shoulder, and then Kyle felt Samuel and Obie half dragging, half carrying him outside as the ceiling started to fall in.

They stood near the curb.

"It's just this house," Berto said, awestruck. "Look across the street."

Kyle spun around. The rest of the neighborhood was unaffected. Palm fronds waved quietly in the night breeze, and lampposts decorated with giant holiday wreaths stayed upright, not even wobbling. No earthquake had sent people running to their front lawns in terror.

"What's happening?" Kyle asked, without expecting an answer. He turned back and froze. Mrs. Caine, now a pallid ghost, peered out at him through the shattered front window, waving good-bye. She mouthed the words *I love you* and faded as the night filled with a roar. After that, the house and everything in it vanished.

Kyle stared at a vacant lot beside the railroad tracks. Wisps of dust rose, and then a breeze stole them away. He bent down and touched the ground, hoping for some clue. The dirt felt hard as rock beneath his fingers. No lush lawn could have grown there without the help of magic.

Samuel looked down at the hard-packed earth. "This ground is so poor you couldn't raise a row with a pitchfork." Then he gazed at Kyle with an odd, wondering expression. "Yet you made it look like grass and—"

"How was I able to create such a huge illusion then, when today I can barely conjure a seagull?" Kyle demanded. He angrily kicked a discarded Coke can and gazed out, searching for some evidence that the house had been there.

Berto placed a hand on Kyle's shoulder. "Kent wasn't the only thing you created. It must have been hard for you as a child."

"I thought Mrs. Caine was real," Kyle replied.

"Her love and devotion were," Obie said.

"You must have been so in need of love that you created the perfect mother," Samuel said wistfully, as though he were thinking of his own home.

"Why didn't everything disintegrate into

ectoplasm, like the seagulls?" Kyle asked after a while. "There should be gobs of that greenish gray stuff all over the lot, everything just vanished."

"Your power was probably immense when you were younger," Obie answered. "But then you must have suppressed your abilities so you could believe your own illusion."

"Loneliness makes us do crazy things," Berto said, as if he knew from personal experience.

Kyle nodded, and swallowed hard to choke off the sob working its way up his throat, but he also wondered if his strange ability could be the reason the government had taken the county to court to seal his case record. Maybe others had witnessed what he had been able to do. He doubted that he would ever know.

"We should start looking for the diamond," Samuel said, halfheartedly brushing his hands across a clump of prickly weeds.

"We're not going to find it," Obie said, sighing heavily as he looked out at the field.

"We have to find it, to fulfill the Legend," Samuel argued.

"I'm tired of being legendary," Kyle said suddenly. "I can't take any more. Not tonight anyway. Let's go to Maddie's party."

Berto started back to the car. "Good idea. I'm not even going to think about Nefandus until morning, and maybe not even then."

It was past midnight when they arrived back at Maddie's house. Kids were gathered on the lawn talking and laughing in small groups. The front door was open, and music drifted outside. Kyle pushed his way through the kids standing on the porch and went inside looking for Emily. He felt someone tap his back and turned.

"Are you the good twin or the bad?" Emily asked, smiling up at him.

"I'm Kyle." He hoped that was the correct answer, because he wanted her to like him.

"I know," she answered and rested her head against his chest. "Ashley told me everything."

"Ashley?" Kyle asked, surprised, and immediately wondered what price he'd have to pay for the favor.

"She said that your twin was trying to

ruin everything between us," Emily confided.

"That's true." Kyle placed his arms around her and pulled her close. The music changed to a slow, soulful song.

The one thing he had wanted all his life was to feel a sense of belonging, and until that moment it was the one thing he had never really had. Now he felt a kinship with his three roommates, a love as close as the love brothers must feel. And he also had a glimmering of hope that maybe he could build a relationship with Emily.

As if to mock him, wind ripped through the front door. The gust twirled about the room, seeking Kyle. He sensed the Fates within the blustery air, taunting him and luring him forward to his unkind destiny.

"Ducunt volentem fata, nolentum trahunt," he whispered, in answer to the wind.

"What?" Emily asked, pulling back and looking up at him.

"It's an old saying in Latin," he explained. "It means, *We can't change the future; it comes to us whether we're prepared or not.*"

Don't miss the next
SONS OF THE DARK book

night sun

THE NEXT DAY, Berto walked down the breezeway at Turney High, toward the quad. The lunch period had started, but no one seemed to be leaving campus. Students were restless, and they had gathered in small groups, talking about the coming solar eclipse. Berto even overheard some of them making wild speculations about satanic cults or alien invasions.

Like everything that happened in L.A., someone had already figured out a way to make money from the recent scares. Most kids had purchased protective charms and crystals from street vendors, and they wore these around their necks. Many had on T-shirts featuring the picture of an eclipsed sun with a caption beneath that read: HAVE YOU BEEN ABDUCTED YET?

Berto found Samuel sitting at a picnic table with Maddie and her best friend, Emily. Samuel was eating a sandwich he'd made from pepperoni and cheese picked off someone else's leftover pizza.

Berto handed him a breath mint. "You have got to find a job," he teased.

Maddie scowled at him.

"What's up?" Berto asked, surprised by her ice-cold reception.

"I can't believe you don't know," Maddie answered. Dark circles were visible beneath her usually vibrant eyes.

"So, tell him," Samuel said, and popped the last bite of sandwich into his mouth.

"Another guy from Turney is missing," she said, in an accusatory voice. "He went to Quake last night and never came home. His mother tried to call him on his cell phone, but all she got was a recording that said he had traveled out of area."

Berto knew she was talking about Pete, but he didn't let on.

"His car was found parked on a side street near the club," Emily added.

"Where were you?" Maddie demanded. "I thought it was your responsibility to—"

"Pete wasn't the only one abducted," Samuel interrupted, gently resting his hand on Maddie's.

"Seven more kids are missing," Emily put in. "Everyone thinks the abductions are related to the solar eclipse, like some cult is involved. My parents won't even let me go out after dark now. . . . Not that I care." She seemed to shudder, as if from a sudden chill, in spite of the warm sunshine.

"I know it's going to turn out to be something even worse than some crazy group with bizarre ideas about satanic rites," Maddie said, and her gaze settled on Berto.

Emily snapped the lid closed on her plastic lunch container. "Whoever it is, I wish the police would catch them soon. I'm scared to sleep alone in my own bedroom."

"It's not something the police are trained to handle," Maddie said with authority.

"Then why aren't you afraid?" Berto asked.

"Maybe you should be the one concerned," Maddie shot back.

"Why should he be?" Samuel asked, becoming defensive on behalf of Berto.

"Because I'm finally going to have the opportunity to prove that there's more to the universe than we perceive with our five senses," she answered.

Berto stared at her blankly. Her tone implied a threat—but what did he have to fear from her?

"You make it sound like Berto is responsible," Samuel said. "Why would you even think that?"

Maddie stood up suddenly, crumpling her lunch bag. "Because . . ." She looked from Berto to Samuel, and back to Berto again.

"Maddie?" Samuel tried to take her hand, but she turned and walked away.